"How miserably things seem to be arranged in this world. If we have no friends, we have no pleasure; and if we have them, we are sure to lose them, and be doubly pained by the loss."

Abraham Lincoln

A GEORGIANA GERMAINE MYSTERY

LITTLE EMPTY PROMISES

CHERYL BRADSHAW

NEW YORK TIMES BEST SELLING AUTHOR

It was a rather cool day in the sleepy town of Cambria, California, the brisk frigidity of fall sweeping through the streets like snow's first drift. Seventy-one-year-old Cordelia Bennett walked up and down the aisles of the local library, feather duster in hand, humming to the tune of Neil Young's "Heart of Gold." It was her fourth day as a library volunteer, and she was grateful for the opportunity. It whisked her away from the quiet of home, a home that held an abundance of bittersweet memories.

One year earlier, Cordelia's husband Marlon had passed away, dashing the plans they'd made to spend their golden years cruising around the world. His illness had been sudden and unexpected, and his death had left her in a state of grief. He'd always been her lifeline, her confidant, the one person who made her feel safe.

She couldn't travel now.

Not without her trusted companion.

It wouldn't be the same.

Nothing would ever be the same again.

Tonight was the first time Cordelia was to close the library on her own, and it was of the utmost importance that everything went to plan. The book drop had been emptied, book returns had been checked in and reshelved, paper had been added to the photocopier and fax machine, and all laptops had been turned off and plugged in for recharging.

As Cordelia did her final rounds, she ran the feather duster along one of the bookshelves, pausing a moment to ingest a lungful of air. Holding the breath a moment, she savored a specific aroma, an aroma only timeless, weathered books could provide. The scent had always reminded her of the subtle fragrance of a candle—earthy with a slight dash of vanilla.

Pleased she'd checked everything off her list, Cordelia grabbed her handbag out of the cubby in the back room and made her way to the front door, stopping to switch off one final light before she departed.

The sound of what Cordelia imagined was a book falling from one of the shelves startled her. She stood a moment in silence, trying to pinpoint which direction it had come from, but the room had returned to silence. Cordelia went aisle to aisle, scanning the floor for any signs of a book, but nothing, it seemed, had come off the shelves.

How odd.

If it isn't a book, what was it?

Taking the inspection a bit further, Cordelia moved to the reading area, thinking she may have overlooked a book left on one of the tables or chairs.

She found nothing.

She walked to the front desk, scanning the counter and the floor around it.

All was in order.

And then she heard something else.

A different sound this time.

Not of something falling.

A sound like ... footsteps.

It couldn't be.

She was alone in the library.

Cordelia had been sure to lock the doors after the last person departed. She'd even checked the handle, ensuring the door was locked.

The moonlight filtered through the window, and Cordelia froze. She could have sworn she'd seen movement on the opposite side of the room. But had she?

"Hello?" she asked. "Is anyone there?"

She'd asked as more of a formality, believing her mind was playing tricks on her, until a shadowy figure stepped out from behind a bookcase.

Stunned, Cordelia said, "You can't be here. The library is closed now. It opens at nine if you wish to return. Come along. I'll let you out."

But the figure didn't 'come along,' as she'd suggested. The figure remained motionless, confusing Cordelia even more. A thought ran through her mind. It was possible she was dealing with a homeless individual who had nowhere to go and, as such, had decided to seek refuge for the evening.

"Excuse me," Cordelia said. "Is there a reason you are refusing to leave? Do you have anywhere else you can go?"

She hoped for an answer this time, but once again, she was met with silence.

A second thought presented itself, one Cordelia didn't want to entertain. It was enough to make her reach into her handbag, taking her time as she fumbled around until she felt the cool steel of her gun. It was the tiniest of things, a gift from Marlon. She'd scoffed when he'd given it to her years before, saying she had no use for a firearm.

Upon bestowing it to her, Marlon had said, "If the need should ever arise, all you have to remember is to point and shoot, dear."

The need had never arisen—until now.

And what's more, the gun had never been fired before.

Cordelia didn't even know what would happen if she tried.

Hands shaking, she raised the gun in front of her, searching for the words she wanted to say.

"I don't know who you are or why you're here, but I'm leaving now," she said.

"You're not going anywhere."

The words had been grunted in such a way to make Cordelia believe the person she was dealing with was going through great effort to mask his voice.

"Like I said, I'm leaving," Cordelia said. "You should do the same."

"What did you see?"

"I beg your pardon?"

"What. Did. You. See?"

"I'm not sure what you're talking about. What did I see ... when?"

"You *know* when."

"I'm afraid not."

"Stop toying with me."

"I can assure you, there's no *toying* involved." There was a click, a sound that made Cordelia fear she wasn't the only one holding a gun. "You should know, I'm armed."

"Makes two of us."

"I'm not afraid to fire, if necessary. Though I'd rather not."

"It's too late."

Too late for what?

With the door to the library locked, Cordelia would have to turn her back on the man to unlock it, a measure too risky to take.

"I see we're at an impasse," she said. "I don't know what I saw or why it's too late. Can we agree to disagree and call it a night?"

"We can call it a night *after* you're dead."

Cordelia replayed the words in her mind a few times, her heart racing as she found herself out of ideas and with nowhere to turn.

"Do you think I'm afraid to die?" she asked. "I'm not."

It was a half-truth at best, but she was hoping to appeal to the intruder's humanity.

Maybe if she could do that, there would still be a way out.

"Ever since my husband died, I've been a shell of a person," she added. "He was my everything. I lived to breathe the air around him. I miss the sound of his voice, the way his smile brightened the darkest of days. And his smell ... I sit in his car sometimes just so I can be reminded of it. Without him, I've struggled to find my way forward. But I believe even in our darkest of days, there is always a way forward. Wouldn't you agree?"

It was quiet for some time, and then there was a loud popping sound, followed by pain ... a stabbing pain in Cordelia's chest.

She sagged to the ground, clutching her heart as she whispered, "I'll be seeing you, Marlon. I'll be seeing you soon."

2

"Mom, did you hear me?" I asked.

My mother shifted her attention from the window to her watch, and then to me, saying, "I ... umm, yeah. Sorry, dear. You mentioned something about a wedding, right?"

"Yeah, *my* wedding."

Her eyes lit up. "*Your* wedding? The two of you set a date, eh? It's about time."

We were standing in my mother's living room, sipping tea, and warming ourselves in front of the fire. It had been a much chillier October than usual. And although I'd always welcomed autumn and the changing of the leaves, I wasn't ready for cooler temperatures just yet.

"We're planning on getting married next year," I said.

"When?"

"August."

My mother raised a brow. "Seems a bit far off, don't you think? Then again, I suppose you've both been married before."

I didn't know what to make of her comment, and I wasn't interested in adding any fuel to the fire, so I said, "It gives us plenty of time to plan. Besides, I've always wanted a summer wedding, and it's not like there's a rush."

"I should say not. It's been over a year since Giovanni's proposal. I was starting to wonder if the two of you would ever tie the knot, or if you'd decided to remain engaged forever."

She was in a testy mood this evening.

Something was bugging her.

I took a sip of tea and let the comment slide.

In truth, I wasn't sure why we'd put off setting a date after our engagement. Months earlier, I'd learned Giovanni had been waiting for me to suggest a timeline for our nuptials. That was when we gave it some serious thought and came up with a plan.

My mother glanced out the window and then back at me again. "Where are you thinking you'll have the ceremony?"

It was a question I expected, but one I wasn't prepared to answer yet.

"New York is a place we've talked about," I said. "It's where we met."

"When you were both in college, and you lived with his sister. I'm aware."

"It holds special meaning to us for that reason. It's also the city where we reunited four years ago."

"It's also where he proposed to you. It doesn't seem like you've only talked about it. It seems like you've decided New York is the place. Am I right?"

I nodded.

She sighed, and I waited for what more she was about to say.

I didn't wait long.

"I'd hoped the two of you would marry here. But I can see why getting married in a place that holds fond memories for the two of you makes sense."

There was disappointment in her eyes when she'd said it, but so far, she wasn't pressing the issue any further.

I was impressed.

"Giovanni's sister, Daniela, has offered to host the wedding and the reception at their family estate," I said. "And before you say anything, I want you to know how important it is to me for you to be involved with as much of the wedding reception planning as you'd like."

"I think I'd like to sit down," she said.

She crossed the room, taking a seat on a chair near the window.

I sat down next to her.

"We're still discussing all the details," I said.

"Is this why you stopped by tonight, to break the news?"

"I spoke to Daniela earlier today, and we discussed a few things, but I wanted to talk to you before any final decisions were made."

"I appreciate the consideration."

And I appreciated how well she was taking it. I'd spent much of the afternoon fretting over the conversation. It was possible I'd worried for nothing, but considering how much more agreeable she was than I'd expected, it gave me pause.

My mother crossed one leg over the other, setting her empty teacup on a side table. "There's something you should know. I met your father in New York City."

"I thought the two of you met here, in Cambria."

"We did, the second time."

"I don't understand."

"After I graduated from high school, I took a trip to New York City with my friend, Cassandra. Her aunt had a home there, and she invited us for a visit. On our third night, we went out to a nightclub, and I met your father."

"If you met in New York City, why did you tell us kids you met in Cambria?"

My mother swished a hand through the air and frowned. "Do you want to hear about it or not?"

"I do."

"Good, then let me talk. I'll explain everything."

I leaned toward her, anxious to hear the rest of the story.

"As I was saying, I first met your father in that New York nightclub. I still remember what he was wearing—a white T-shirt under a black leather jacket. Jeans rolled up at the bottom. The moment our eyes met, he smiled, and walked right over to me."

"What did he say?"

"He told me his name was Abe and that I was the prettiest gal he'd ever laid eyes on. While Cassandra tore it up on the dance floor with a gentleman she'd just met, I sat at a booth with your father. We talked for over three hours."

"What about?"

"Lots of things, and at the end of the conversation, he told me he was only in the city for the night. The next morning, he was flying to Spain to study abroad for a while. Before we said our goodbyes, he asked for my address and said he would write to me."

"And did he?" I asked.

"Every week for a year. And then ... I ... we ..." She bit down on her lip, crossing her arms in front of her. "I'm ashamed about what happened next, you see."

"Why? What happened?"

"For the first six months, I wrote back to every letter he sent. And then ... well, I met someone else. Your father continued to send letters each week, but I stopped replying to them. A few months later, things fizzled out with the other guy. I thought about writing your father to explain why I'd stopped corresponding, but I was embarrassed. I couldn't bring myself to do it."

It was hard for me to believe my mother had ever been embarrassed about anything.

"The second time you met was here," I said, intrigued. "How did that happen?"

"As soon as your father returned from Spain, he came straight to Cambria. He knocked on my door, and when I opened it, he handed me the most beautiful bouquet I'd ever seen, and he professed his love for me. I didn't know what to say. I stood there for a moment and then I burst into tears. I realized I loved him too."

"Why did you feel like you couldn't tell us kids the real story until now? We would have understood."

She reached out, taking my hand. "I know that now. I should have been honest about it from the start. I felt awful about how I'd handled everything with your father. After your father and I talked, and I explained what had happened, he was disappointed at first. Then he suggested we start from scratch, and that's just what we did."

"What matters is you found your way back to each other in the end."

"Just like you and Giovanni. I suppose now you can see why New York is a special place for me too."

She released my hand and squinted, peering out the window for a third time.

Then there was another quick glance at the time.

"You've been looking out the window and then at your watch a lot since I've been here. Is everything okay?"

She tapped a finger to her lips. "Mmmph, I don't know. Cordelia's porch light is on."

I glanced out the window, staring at the house my mother was pointing at.

"Why are you concerned about your neighbor's porch light?" I asked.

"She always leaves it on when she's not home in the evening, and she always turns it off when she gets back. It's getting late. The light's still on, and she should have been home a while ago."

"Maybe she got tied up running errands."

"I think I'll give her a call."

My mother removed her cell phone from her pocket and dialed.

There was no answer.

"Well, I just don't understand it, don't understand it at all, I tell you," my mother said. "Cordelia doesn't leave the house much. Not since her husband passed away."

"How's she doing?"

"Depressed. Yessiree, that one word just about sums it up. I was visiting with her a few weeks ago, and she made a comment about having nothing to live for now that he's gone. She has no children and not much family to speak of, other than a sister whom she hasn't spoken to in years."

"Do the two of you get together often?"

"I pop in a couple of times a week to see how she's doing. During one of my recent visits, I told her I knew what she was going through, having lost your father some time ago. I promised her it would get better. Perhaps it was a promise I ought not to have made."

"Why?"

"Part of me worries I've pushed her back into society before she's ready. As I thought of ways to help her cope with his death, I came up with what I thought was a brilliant idea. Cordelia loves books of all genres. Her house is filled to the brim with them. I knew the local library was looking for a volunteer, and I proposed it would be a perfect opportunity for her to dip a toe back into the outside world."

"What did she think about your suggestion?"

"She loved the idea. She worked there today, in fact. I'm

concerned because the library closed a few hours ago. I don't understand why she isn't home yet."

"You said she loves books. Maybe she stayed late to read."

"Cordelia doesn't like to be out after dark. She's a bit funny that way. Why would she stay when she could just bring the book home?"

It was a fair point.

"If it will make you feel better, we can head over to the library and see if she's still there," I said.

My mother nodded and bolted from the chair. "It would make me feel better, yes. I'll grab my shawl and meet you at the car in a jiffy."

There were no lights on inside the library when we arrived, and Cordelia's car was still parked out front, a fact I found strange. We parked, walked up to the front door, and I reached out, twisting the knob.

I expected it to be locked.

It wasn't.

Even stranger.

"If I was worried before, I'm even more worried now," my mother said.

We entered the library, and I pointed at the floor. "Someone's dropped their keys."

My mother cupped a hand to the side of her mouth and said, "Yoo-hoo, Cordelia, are you here?"

We were met with silence.

I ran a hand along the wall, stopping when I located the light switch. I flipped it on and looked around. There was no sign of Cordelia at first, but the local library was small. If she was here, it wouldn't take long to find her.

"Let's do a quick walkthrough," I said.

My mother nodded, and we made our way over to the bookshelves, going up and down the aisles, searching for Cordelia. I'd rounded the fourth aisle when I saw someone not too far from me, and I gasped. Hunched over on the floor several feet away was an older woman, turned on her side.

Blood was everywhere.

On her clothes.

On the carpet.

A gun on the floor next to her.

My mother caught up to me, followed my line of sight, and shrieked, racing over to the woman as she dropped to her knees.

She reached out, shaking her.

"Mom," I said. "I don't think you should—"

"Cordelia, it's Darlene. I'm here. Open your eyes! Please, *please* open your eyes!"

I walked over and kneeled next to Cordelia, feeling for a pulse. It seemed like there was one, but if I was right, it was faint. I placed my ear above her mouth, surprised when I felt a tingling sensation of hot air.

"I think ... it's faint, but I believe she's still breathing," I said.

"You think she's still alive?"

"I hope so."

As my heart pulsated inside my chest, I called for an ambulance.

My mother began sobbing, patting Cordelia's hand, as she begged her friend to "hang in there," telling her "help is on the way."

I gave the 9-1-1 operator details about where we were and what we knew, which wasn't much and then I ended the call. I was anxious to take a closer look at Cordelia before anyone else arrived.

She'd been shot in the chest, which in my mind meant one of two things:

One, the wound she'd sustained had been self-inflicted.

Or two, and what seemed more logical, Cordelia had been attacked, shot, and left for dead.

"If someone else is responsible for what happened here tonight, this is a crime scene," I said. "We need to be careful not to touch anything until the police get here."

"Well, of course someone shot her. What other explanation could there be?"

My mother sprang to a standing position. "I'm going to check the bathroom, see if there's a first aid kit."

"Mom, let me look around the place first. If she was attacked, whoever did this to her might still be here."

My mother reached into her handbag, pulling out a pistol. "Don't you worry about me. I've been going to the gun range for a few years now. If the person who did this to her is still around, he'll wish he wasn't. Get Foley on the horn. He needs to be here."

Foley was the next call on my list. He was the chief of police for San Luis Obispo County, and he was also married to my sister.

He answered on the second ring, saying, "It's not like you to call this late. Everything okay?"

"It's not."

"What's going on?"

"I'm at the local library with my mother."

"Hasn't it closed by now?"

"Her neighbor just started volunteering here, and she's been shot."

"Shot? Is she dead or alive?"

"She's breathing, but it's faint. I'll explain more when you get here."

"Hold tight. I'll call Whitlock, and we'll be right there."

The call ended, and I glanced down at Cordelia. Her eyes

flashed open. She looked at me and whispered, "Marlon, my darling, you're here. I knew you'd come."

"It's not Marlon. It's Georgiana Germaine, Darlene's daughter. Can you tell me what happened to you?"

She seemed to have not heard me at all—or was ignoring the question. "We're together now, Marlon. Together forever, just like I always knew we would be."

As my mother raced back to my side, first aid kit in hand, Cordelia's eyes closed, and what little life she had left closed along with her.

"Is she ... she's not ... she's going to be okay, right?" my mother asked. "We can fix this ... we can make it better."

I bent down, checking Cordelia's pulse a second time, and then I glanced up at my mother. "I'm sorry. It's too late, Mom. We're too late. She's ... she's dead."

4

While I waited for everyone to arrive, I did a quick scan of a few sections of the library. I found nothing, and no one. Foley pulled to a screeching stop, and he and Whitlock got out. I walked over to meet them.

Amos Whitlock was a detective for the county, working under Foley. He'd worked alongside my father in his younger years. Bored in retirement, he'd jumped at the chance to return to detective work when a position opened, and given I was a private investigator, our paths often crossed when my agency was hired to investigate homicide cases.

Whitlock ran a hand through his sleek, silver hair and gave me a nod. "Evening, Georgiana. Nice to see you ... well, it *is* nice to see you, just not under these circumstances."

"Nice to see you too."

Though the hour was late, he was still looking fashionable in a light blue shirt and fitted black slacks. He was wearing his signature dress shoes, which were buffed to a shine—I was sure I could see my reflection in them if I tried.

Foley, on the other hand, looked a little worse for wear.

He noticed me eyeing him and said, "I ... ahh, I was in my pajamas, watching a movie with your sister when you called."

"I didn't say anything," I said.

"There's no need. You've never had even the slightest hint of a poker face. Your expression said it for you. Now, fill me in. Start by explaining how you and your mother stumbled upon her neighbor and what you know about what happened here tonight."

"I was at my mother's house earlier this evening, and she noticed Cordelia hadn't returned home after work. She was worried, so we decided to drive over here and see if we could find her. When we first got here, she was still alive, but she died within minutes of our arrival."

"You note the exact time of death?"

"Of course I did—8:22 p.m. on the dot."

"Was she conscious at all before she passed?"

"Yes and no. She didn't offer any information about what happened here tonight, but she whispered something about seeing her husband again. Then she passed away."

"Take me to her."

Foley and Whitlock followed me to the other side of the room. As soon as my mother spotted them, she rushed over to Whitlock, throwing her arms around him.

"It's just awful, and it's all my fault," she said. "I'm the one who pushed Cordelia to take this job. I thought it would be good for her. If it wasn't for me, she'd still be alive."

Whitlock patted her on the back and said, "Now, now ... it's not your fault. You were just trying to be a good friend."

"Who would want to harm such a sweet, innocent old woman?" my mother asked. "Who would do such a thing?"

"Hard to say, but we'll get to the bottom of it."

"We will," Foley added. "You look tired, Darlene. You should go home and get some rest."

"I'd like to stay, thank you," my mother said.

"It's going to be a long night," Foley said. "There's no reason for you to stick around. I'll call you in the morning, okay?"

My mother looked at me and said, "Come on, then. Let's leave them to it."

I shook my head. "I'd like to stay, Mom. I texted Harvey, and he's on his way to pick you up."

Harvey was my stepfather, and the county's former chief of police. He'd also worked with my father back in the day and had been his closest friend. Decades earlier, after my father died, Harvey stepped in, making frequent stops at our house to ensure we had everything we needed. My mother leaned on him for support, and after a time, they developed feelings for each other.

I'd never questioned my mother's love for Harvey. But my father's death left a gaping hole in her heart, a hole that grew larger whenever she lost someone close. She'd been a lot quieter tonight, which wasn't like her usual boisterous self. Knowing she was in for a tough, emotional night, I'd texted Harvey.

He arrived a few minutes later, said a quick hello, and then ushered my mother out the door. As they made their exit, Silas walked in. He was the county medical examiner and a good friend. His long, sun-kissed blond locks had been pulled back into a manbun, and he was dressed like a Hawaiian tourist, in a wrinkled floral shirt and khaki shorts.

He spotted me and walked over.

"Hey, rough night, eh?" Silas said. "Who died?"

"An older woman," I said. "She was my mother's neighbor."

"Oh, wow. That's too bad. Does your mother know?"

"We were the ones who found her."

"How'd it happen?"

"Gunshot wound."

"You get a good look at her?"

"I did, and the first thing I want to know is whether the gunshot wound is self-inflicted or if someone shot her."

Silas nodded and looked around. "You find a shell casing?"

"Not so far. When we got here, there was a gun on the floor not far from her body. It's small, though. Looks more like a toy. Reminded me of the gun John Wilkes Booth used when he shot Lincoln. If it was self-inflicted, a suicide, which doesn't sit well with me, she would have had to know the exact spot she needed to shoot herself to make sure the deed was done."

"Huh. She was only shot once then?"

"Yeah," I said. "She was alive when I found her."

"For how long?"

"A few minutes." I glanced at my watch. "She died about an hour and forty minutes ago. I can give you the exact time."

"Good to know. I'll have a look, see if anything stands out."

He left my side and made his way over to Foley, who was standing beside Cordelia. Whitlock was walking up and down the book aisles, whistling, something he often did at a crime scene. According to him, it helped him stay calm and focused. In an abrupt manner, the whistling stopped, and Whitlock shouted, "Hey guys. I think I found something."

The "something" Whitlock found was a crumpled-up sticky note, which wasn't all that unusual given we were in a library. Written on the note was a description I found curious:

Short curly hair
70s
Glasses

"Could mean something, could mean nothing," Whitlock said. "Hard to say."

"It describes Cordelia to a T," I said.

"How many people work here?" Foley asked. "Any idea?"

"I'm not sure. It's a small library. Maybe a couple of employees and one or two volunteers."

Foley turned toward me. "The key ring you found ... If she was attacked, I was hoping it had fallen from the assailant's pocket. Turns out one of the keys unlocks the door to the library, and another unlocks Cordelia's car."

"She must have dropped them on her way out, or when she realized she wasn't alone," I said.

Whitlock moved a hand to his hip. "A library seems like such a strange place for a murder. Wouldn't you agree?"

"*If* she was murdered," I said.

"Sure looks like murder to me," Foley said. "What makes you believe otherwise?"

"Oh, I don't. I was just thinking about something my mother said to me today. Cordelia made a comment to her about not having anything to live for after her husband died. I'm not saying her loneliness caused her to kill herself, and the whole idea doesn't work for me. But it does need to be ruled out."

"Guess we'll have to wait and see what Silas has to say on the matter after he examines the scene and conducts the autopsy. Until then, it's fair to assume foul play was involved."

"I agree."

I heard a sharp rapping sound, and in unison, our heads turned. In the dim glow of the library's porch light, a woman stood at the threshold, knocking on the doorjamb. She was dressed in a long nightgown with a puffy coat over it. In her hand was a hot fudge sundae.

Foley cupped a hand to the side of his mouth and shouted, "Library's closed, ma'am. You'll have to come back another day."

"I know it's closed," the woman said. "I work here. What I don't know is what *you* are all doing here at this hour."

Foley, Whitlock, and I exchanged glances.

"What do you think?" I asked.

"I think we should talk to her," Whitlock said. "What say you, Foley?"

"She's not coming in here and messing with my crime scene," Foley said.

"I'm not saying we should let her in," Whitlock said. "I'm saying we should talk to her."

"Go on, then," Foley said. "But I don't want her stepping a single foot inside this place."

Whitlock saluted and said, "Roger that."

He started for the front door, and I followed, half expecting Foley to stop me, but he didn't.

Whitlock grinned at the woman and said, "Hello there. Mind if we talk outside?"

"Of course, I mind," she said. "It's cold out here. Let me in."

"It is a wee bit nippy, isn't it? How about we hop in my SUV? It has the works—heated seats, a blanket in the back, everything to get you warm in no time."

The woman raised a brow, confused. "I want to know what's going on here. Why won't you let me in?"

"We're investigating an incident that happened earlier this evening."

"What are you talking about? What *incident*? Who are you two?"

"My name is Georgiana Germaine," I said. "And this is Detective Whitlock. What's your name?"

"Samantha Swan. I manage the library, and you still haven't answered my question."

"Come with me, and let's get warmed up," Whitlock said. "I'll answer whatever questions I can."

She hesitated a moment, taking a few bites of the sundae, which had all but melted. Then she nodded, and we followed Whitlock to his SUV. My buns were cold, and as soon as I hopped into the back seat, and he started the vehicle, I cranked the seat warmer all the way up.

"Forgive my appearance," Samantha said. "I was at home, planning on making it an early night, and I had a craving for something sweet. So I threw on my coat and left, thinking I wouldn't run into anyone while I was out. Well, no one except for an employee at the drive-thru."

"We've all been there," Whitlock said. "How long have you known Cordelia Bennett?"

"She's been a patron of the library for decades. For years, she'd come in once or twice a month and read to the kids on the weekend. We just brought her on as a volunteer. I'd hoped it might cheer her up after the loss of her husband. Why do you ask?"

I waited to see how Whitlock would respond, knowing the truth of what happened tonight would be public knowledge soon enough.

"I don't know how else to say it, so I'm just going to be straight with you," Whitlock said.

"Please do."

"Mrs. Bennett is dead."

"What? How? Where?"

"She died in the library sometime this evening."

Samantha gasped, slapping a hand against her mouth, her head shaking. "No, no, no, no, no. I don't believe it. I *can't* believe it. I saw her earlier today, and we talked. What happened?"

"We're not sure yet. That's what we're trying to figure out."

"Is she ... still in there?"

"For now."

"How did she die? Was it a heart attack or something?"

Whitlock went quiet for a time, running a hand along his chin, thinking. "What I am about to say won't be easy for you to hear, I imagine. Since you're the one who runs things at the library, I feel it best you know the truth. She sustained a gunshot wound."

Whitlock's comment gave Samantha such a shock, the sundae she was holding slipped from her hands, peppering the back seat in a sticky coat of melted vanilla and hot fudge—now, cold fudge.

She reached for the door handle, saying, "I ... I have to go. I can't ... I don't ... I don't want to be here."

I placed a hand on her arm. "Please, wait just a minute. It's a lot to process. I know. We're going to figure out what happened tonight and why. Rest assured."

Through tear-filled eyes, Samantha said, "Cordelia was one of the nicest people I've ever met. I can't believe it. I can't believe she's dead. What if I'd stayed tonight, and if Cordelia had gone home? Would it have been me instead of her?"

Given the note Whitlock had found, and the fact we believed Cordelia had been murdered, the attack seemed to have been a targeted one. The description on the paper seemed too perfect of a match to Cordelia to suggest otherwise. One thought led to another, and I wondered ... Were we looking at a murder for hire?

"I know this news is difficult to take in," Whitlock said, "but it would be a big help to us if you'd stay a few minutes longer so we can ask you a few questions."

Samantha nodded, reaching into her handbag and pulling out a tissue. She blotted her eyes and sniffled, seeming to regain her composure. "Sure, of course I can stay. Anything I can do to help."

Whitlock grinned, pleased with her answer. "What time did you speak with Mrs. Bennett today?"

"Oh, it was right before I left, so I'd say a little after four this afternoon."

"How did she seem when you talked to her?"

"She was in the best of spirits, much happier than I'd seen her in some time."

"What did the two of you talk about?"

Samantha tapped a finger against the armrest, thinking. "It was Cordelia's first time closing the library, and she wanted to go over everything with me to make sure she got it all right."

"Is it common for a volunteer to close?"

Samantha looked down, going quiet for a time.

"It isn't," she said. "I'll admit, I was supposed to close tonight, but my granddaughter had a volleyball game this afternoon. I was telling Cordelia about it, and I mentioned how much I wished I could be there. She offered to close for me. I suppose I should have given it a bit more thought, but I was too excited about making the game to think much of it."

"How many employees and volunteers work here?"

"Johnny Mansfield is an employee, and Cordelia is ... *was* our only volunteer. We had one other volunteer, but she moved away a few months ago." Samantha glanced toward the library, placing a hand over her forehead like a visor. "I don't ... I don't want to see ... I don't know how I'm ever going to be able to step foot in there after what's happened. I suppose we'll need to close for a while. What's the process like? How long will it take?"

"I can't answer that right now," Whitlock said. "It depends on several things. For one, the chief of police needs to be satisfied that we've gathered all the relevant evidence and we've done all we can here."

"It's surreal. Even after hearing it from your lips, I still can't believe it."

"We appreciate you taking the time to talk to us tonight. Why don't you leave me your contact information? I'll be in touch when I have more news to share."

Samantha nodded, and Whitlock put her information into his phone.

She blotted her eyes a few more times, and I said, "I'm sorry about your friend."

"I am too."

She reached for the door handle once more.

"Would you mind answering one last question?" I asked.

"Sure. What is it?"

"Do you wear glasses?"

"Sometimes."

"You're not wearing them right now, though."

"I don't need to wear them all the time. My distance vision is excellent. It's the things that are close that give me trouble. Can't read the back of a soup can to save my life."

I knew just how she felt.

Over the last few years, my near vision had begun to decline.

"Would you mind telling me your age?" I asked.

"That seems like an odd question. Why do you want to know?"

"I'm just curious."

Whitlock turned, eyeing me like he was trying to figure out why I'd asked, but he remained quiet.

"I'll be sixty-nine next month," she said. "Can I go now?"

"Sure," I said.

"I'm so sorry about the mess I made."

Whitlock shrugged. "Don't worry about it. My vehicle is due for a cleaning, and now I have a reason not to keep putting it off."

Samantha nodded and opened the door, blowing her nose into a tissue as she waved to us and headed to her car.

As she drove away, Whitlock turned to me. "Penny for your thoughts?"

"Based on the note you found and what was written on it, I'd first suspected Cordelia's death may have been premeditated, that she was targeted somehow. Let's say I'm right, and the note was left by the killer. It gives a description of a person who's short, with curly hair, in their 70s, with glasses. At first glance, it's easy to assume it's a description of Cordelia because she's dead. But she wasn't supposed to be here tonight, closing the library. Samantha had been scheduled to close. When we were talking to her just now, it occurred to me that she also fits the description written on the sticky note." I shrugged. "I don't know. It's like you say—maybe the note means something and maybe it doesn't."

"I want to believe it does."

I did too.

I also believed it was possible someone had been hired to commit the murder.

The question was—*why?*

6

It had been two weeks since Cordelia's death, and Foley and Whitlock hadn't gotten much further in their investigation. Silas had finished his postmortem examination and confirmed the gun found next to Cordelia's body contained bullets, but they were much smaller than the one recovered from her body. She had been shot with a different gun, a bigger gun with bigger bullets. And based on the bullet's trajectory, it was impossible for her death to have been a suicide.

Many questions remained, pressing against the police investigation like a weighted blanket:

Who wanted to kill Cordelia, and why?

Was Cordelia the intended target?

Or was the bullet intended for someone else, a case of mistaken identity?

Was this the work of a hit man, a hired killer?

The who, what, and why of it all had flooded my thoughts in the days following her death. In speaking with my mother about Cordelia in recent days, I'd learned Cordelia was a simple woman who led a quiet life, both before and after her husband's death. She wasn't the type of person to make enemies. She had always been thought of as somewhat of a reclusive introvert by her neighbors. After Marlon's death, she was even more so.

As for her murder, Foley wanted to lean into the theory that she'd been at the wrong place at the wrong time, and that she may not have been the intended target. They'd spoken to Samantha a couple more times, but their theory couldn't be proven. I was still of the notion that the murder had been premeditated—whether Cordelia was the target, Samantha, or someone else entirely. I just couldn't come up with a logical reason as to why just yet. Not that I *was* trying to come up with one. It wasn't my investigation, so for now, I sat back, checking in with Foley and Whitlock here and there to see where they were at with everything.

As I sat at my desk on a cool weekday morning, pondering on stepping out and grabbing a snack and a hot drink, the office door opened. I looked over, eyeing the woman who'd just walked in. She had short, black hair, and her lips were painted with bright-red lipstick. I guessed she was in her upper seventies, and she was dressed like she'd just stepped out of an Old Hollywood movie—wearing a fitted black dress, and not one, but two strands of pearls around her neck.

She glanced at me and said, "Hello, I'd like to speak with whoever's in charge here."

"Depends on what services you need," I said. "I'm Georgiana Germaine, the owner of Case Closed Detective Agency. I work alongside Lilia Hunter and Simone Bonet. Hunter locates missing persons, does background checks, and that sort of thing. Simone does surveillance work and assists me in homicide cases. What can I do for you?"

The woman took a seat on a chair opposite my desk and crossed one leg over the other. "My name is Claudette Carrington, and I'd like to hire you to find out who killed my sister."

"Who's your sister?"

"Cordelia Bennett."

I leaned back in my chair, sizing her up and down. She was much different than Cordelia in appearance, her opposite in every way.

"Cordelia was my mother's neighbor," I said. "She lived across the street from her."

"Who is your mother?"

"Darlene Germaine."

Claudette rolled her eyes but said nothing.

"I take it the two of you have met," I said.

"We have, this morning, right before I came to see you. She's ... I'm not sure how to put it."

"Put it any way you like."

"She asks a lot of questions, to say the least."

"My mother and your sister were good friends."

"Yes, your mother told me as much. She was the one who suggested my sister volunteer at the library. Was she not?"

Claudette's tone was accusatory, almost like she thought my mother held some blame in her sister's death.

"What's your point?" I asked.

Claudette looked me in the eye and grinned. "You're a feisty one, aren't you?"

"I can be."

"I wasn't suggesting my sister died because your mother convinced her to volunteer."

"Weren't you?"

"No matter how it happened or why it happened, what's done is done. I'm here because I need to know who did it, and I've been told you have a great track record for solving murders."

I did.

An impeccable one.

I leaned back, tapping my finger on the desktop, thinking.

If I was to take her case, which I had to admit, I'd been hoping to get involved with in some way, I had questions.

"When's the last time you spoke to your sister?" I asked.

"I fail to see how my relationship with Cordelia has any bearing on her murder."

"I'm thorough," I said. "I like to know everything. Even things that turn out to be irrelevant. It's part of what makes me good at my job."

Claudette reached inside her handbag, glancing at me as she said, "Mind if I smoke?"

"Not at all. Feel free to smoke outside. We can talk more when you're finished."

She huffed a disappointed sigh. "To answer your question, I don't know when we last spoke to one another."

"Was it days before she died? Months? Years?"

I knew the answer to the question.

I just wanted to hear what Claudette would say.

"It's been years since we talked last."

"Why so long?" I asked.

"It's rather complicated."

"I have time."

"Yeah, well, I don't like talking about it."

"How about giving me a brief summary?"

There was a long pause.

Claudette looked at me.

I looked at her.

And I waited.

"All right, fine, if I must," she said. "My sister married the man I loved. Is that brief enough for you?"

"It's a start. How long ago?"

"It's been many decades ago now."

"I can't imagine how hard it must have been on you."

"Marlon was the man I thought I was going to go through life with, and then ..."

She allowed the words to trail off, staring at me like she was finished discussing the matter, and then she had a change of heart.

"I introduced Marlon to Cordelia, and that was it," she said. "Of course, the two of them spent their entire relationship apologizing to me. They said things like, 'Oh, we didn't expect it to happen. It just did,' and 'We never meant to hurt you.' They seemed to think all would be forgiven, that I'd wish them well and be fine with it. I was livid. I'm *still* livid."

"Did you ever move on, date anyone else or get married?"

She twisted her lips into a wry grin. "Oh, I've had numerous flings over the years. But flings were all they were. There was a certain kind of passion with Marlon that I never found in anyone else, not that he felt the same. I suppose I convinced myself back then that he returned my feelings. It was foolish of me. I see that now."

"When did you learn Marlon had passed away?"

"Cordelia reached out to me right before his funeral. It was the first time I'd heard from her in many years. I suppose she decided she'd apologized enough to me, and at some point, she just gave up."

"When she contacted you, did the two of you speak?"

"She wrote me a letter. I'll admit, I read it. I was curious to know what she had to say. I thought she'd be back to apologizing again, but instead she ..."

"She?" I prompted, anxious for her to say more.

Claudette pulled a cigarette case and a lighter out of her handbag. "Forgive me. If I'm to continue, I need a moment."

She stood and started for the door.

I followed, wanting to keep her talking.

Once outside, Claudette lit the cigarette, slid it into her mouth, and turned, surprised to see me standing beside her.

She held the cigarette case out to me. "Care to join?"

"No, thank you."

"Then why have you accompanied me?"

"I'm a little impatient, I suppose. I'd like to know more about what your sister's letter said."

"In short, there were no apologies, no regrets. With Marlon gone, she was sad and depressed. She felt alone, and while she expressed interest in us patching things up and leaving the past behind, she was angry and disappointed with how I'd refused to relent after all these years. I could tell."

"How did the letter end?"

"She asked if there was anything she could do to make things right between us. She told me she loved me and always had."

"Did you write her back?"

"I did not."

Though stoic since she'd first walked through the door, Claudette was beginning to crack, the armor she'd been shielding herself with chipping away. I could hear it in her voice, see it in her expression, and in her eyes, which were pooling with tears.

"You regret not writing her back," I said. "I can tell."

"I regret nothing."

"There's no reason not to admit it to me. I'm not here to judge you. I'm here to listen."

"To what? The sound of an old woman yammering on about things she cannot change?"

Things she cannot change.

She could have been referring to her refusal to make things right with her sister. But I believed there was something more, a deep-seated guilt, a guilt that drove her to me today. If she didn't care, she wouldn't have bothered.

"Why are you here, Claudette?" I asked. "What made you decide to hire me?"

"I already told you. I want you to find the person who murdered my sister." She slid the cigarette case inside her bag. "Name your price."

"It depends."

"On what?"

"When I take on a client, I want to feel confident they are being transparent with me."

"Are you implying I'm not?"

"I'm implying there's something you aren't telling me," I said.

Claudette shook her head and flicked the butt of her cigarette on the ground, snuffing it out with the heel of her red-bottom Louboutin shoe. "I'm not making an effort to keep things from you."

"But you are."

"It's more complicated than you know."

"Complicated how?"

"What if I told you my sister died because of me? What if I told you that *I* am responsible for her murder?"

7

"I would say I didn't believe you," I said. "If you were responsible for your sister's death, why would you come here today, telling me you wanted me to find the person who killed her?"

We were back inside the office, sitting at my desk.

"Responsibility comes in many forms," Claudette said. "There are more ways to kill a person than with a bullet through the heart."

"Care to explain?"

Claudette folded one hand over the other, resting them on her lap. "When I didn't respond to my sister's first letter, she sent me a second one. It arrived a few days before she died. I'm sorry to admit I didn't read it. Well, I read it, but not until after I heard she was dead."

"Tell me about the second letter."

"It was a continuation of what she'd said in her first letter, all except for the end. She made a comment about fearing for her life. At the time, I assumed she was being dramatic. I interpreted it to mean she feared living a life without Marlon in it. Now I'm concerned I may have been incorrect in my thinking."

"Why?"

"When we were young, long before Marlon came into the picture, we were close. We grew up with nothing. Our parents couldn't scrape two pennies together, which isn't to say they didn't do all they could for us. They were hard times. When it came to entertainment, we had to create it for ourselves. I suppose it's the reason my sister loved books and libraries. The library was a place she could go to get away from reality, a place she could create a world of her own. She was always a bit shy, and the library was a quiet place where she could sit and observe others without them noticing, something she's always liked to do."

She seemed to be steering me in a direction, but which direction we were headed in, I wasn't sure.

"Are you saying your sister was an eavesdropper or observant or ...?" I asked.

"She used to take notes about things she saw and overheard. I bet she knew more about the people in this town than they knew about themselves, and because she was the quiet sort, she often blended into the background, went unnoticed."

"When she took notes, where did she keep them?"

"In a notebook. Now, I have no way of knowing whether she continued to observe and write things down after we'd parted ways, but I'm inclined to believe she did."

"The police haven't mentioned anything about finding any notes she may have written," I said.

"It doesn't mean they didn't. Maybe they did, and they didn't tell you."

She was right, though I felt certain Foley or Whitlock would have mentioned it to me if they had.

"You said you were at your sister's house this morning," I said. "Did you find anything or see anything I should know about?"

"I did not. I ... it was the first time I've stepped foot inside her house."

"I can't imagine what it must have been like."

"Do you know she had an entire wall in her hallway dedicated to photos of us throughout the years?"

"I did. My mother mentioned it to me."

"I spent so many years rejecting her, not allowing her back into my heart, and all along she was honoring the history we shared together. I'll bet she thought I'd come around, but I never did. I don't believe I'll ever forgive myself for that. We always assume we have time to make things right, to right our wrongs, but time has a funny way of slipping through our fingers. We blink, and it's run out, and there's not a thing we can do to get it back."

She flicked a single tear from her eye, and I grabbed a tissue, handing it to her.

She waved it away. "I'm fine. My sister left everything to me, you know, in her will."

"I didn't know."

"It's one of the reasons I'm here. Her estate lawyer phoned and asked me to meet with him. After Marlon died, she changed her will, leaving everything, all her assets to me."

"Did she mention it in the letters she wrote you?"

"She did not." Claudette reached inside her handbag, pulling out a couple of envelopes secured together with a rubber band. She slapped them down on the desk in front of me. "These are the letters my sister sent me before she died. See for yourself."

I removed the rubber band from the envelopes, took the letters out, and glanced over each one. Claudette was right. There was no mention of Cordelia leaving anything to her sister in her will. Had she done so, it would have been easy for me to consider Claudette a suspect. But she didn't strike me as a woman who wanted for anything.

"Do you mind if I make a copy of these?" I asked.

Claudette swished a hand through the air. "I have no use for them. They're yours to keep. I've given a lot of thought to my sister's murder, and I don't believe it was happenstance. It's my opinion that she saw or overheard something she shouldn't have, and she was killed for it."

"I've had the same thoughts."

"I spoke to the police before I came here. They have no leads and no suspects, which is frustrating. It's why I've come to you. I'd like to speed this process along. What do you think? Will you take the case or not?"

Since Cordelia's death, I'd spoken to Foley about the investigation a couple of times, trying not to be too intrusive with my questions, which for me, wasn't easy. I preferred to be in on the action, and with Claudette sitting in front of me, offering to pay me for the privilege, the decision was an easy one.

"I will take your case," I said. "I'll meet with my team, give them the details, and we'll start looking into it today."

8

"Why is it every time a murder investigation comes along, you find a way to get involved?"

Foley was standing behind his desk, staring out the office window, shaking his head.

"Hey, Claudette came to me," I said. "She's Cordelia's sister."

"Of course she did. And I'll just bet Darlene put her up to it."

"Even if you're right, it doesn't mean my mother thinks you're incapable of solving Cordelia's murder. I suppose she thinks we make a stronger team when we work together."

"A team, huh? You know, all of this would have been a whole lot easier if you would have just come back to work as a detective."

"It's a whole lot easier to work for myself," I said. "No offense."

"What's *easier* is that working for yourself has made you believe you can justify breaking the rules."

I crossed one leg over the other. "Within reason."

Whitlock, who was standing by the door, arms crossed, chimed in with, "Not that anyone asked me, but I think working together on this investigation, or any murder investigation, is a swell idea. Georgiana's got the same knack for solving murders that her father had."

"You're right," Foley said. "No one asked you."

Foley's demeanor was off today, and not by a little—by a lot.

I was used to getting a little pushback from him, but not as much as he was giving me now.

"What's going on with you?" I asked.

"Why do you assume something's going on?"

"You're giving me a lot more flack than usual," I said.

"Maybe more flack is what you need," he said. "You ever think of that?"

Whitlock and I exchanged worried glances, and I went quiet, trying to make sense of the changing tide and what I was going to do about it.

Whitlock thumbed toward the hallway. "I'm gonna go ... and, ahh, yeah, get a cup of coffee. Give the two of you a chance to talk."

He walked out, closing the door behind him.

Gee, thanks.

Leave me with Grumpy McGrump Face in my time of need.

Foley looked at me, and I looked at him, and he hunched over, arms stretched out, pressing his hands onto his desk. He closed his eyes and huffed a long sigh.

"I've always come to you when I've been hired to investigate a murder, offering to share information and suggesting we work together," I said. "I don't know what more to say. Cordelia's sister asked if I would take the case, and I said yes."

"You've said what you wanted to say. There isn't anything more to discuss."

Knowing the next thing I had queued up to come out of my mouth wouldn't bode well for either one of us, I stood, heading for the door while I still maintained the slightest sense of decorum.

"If you want to talk about my conversation with Cordelia's sister sometime, let me know," I said. "I have other places to be right now."

"Hang on a minute, Georgiana. Don't go."

"I don't have it in me to continue this conversation. If you're going to keep talking to me the way you have been, I'm done listening. I can only hold my tongue for so long, a fact you well know. Do yourself a favor and ... you know, stop before you push me too far."

"I'm not ... I didn't mean to upset you. It's not you I'm angry with, all right? I have a lot on my mind."

I had a hand on the doorknob.

Leaving would be easy.

But everything in me said staying was what he needed right now.

I turned.

"Care to talk about whatever's going on with you?" I asked. "You're upset about something—it's obvious."

Foley seemed to be considering the olive branch I'd extended.

"Maybe later," he said. "I would like to know what the sister had to say. Stay for a bit, and I promise to make up for my previous behavior."

He took a seat at his desk, and I remained standing, leaning against the wall as I thought about where to begin. "Cordelia wrote her sister a couple of letters before she died. Did you know?"

"Nope. Go on."

"She read the first one and didn't respond, and then she received a second one close to the time Cordelia was murdered. She didn't read it until after she learned Cordelia was dead." I reached into my handbag, pulling out the envelopes Claudette had given to me. "I want to keep these, but you can make copies."

He glanced at the envelopes. "What's in the letters?"

"Before I get into the letters, you should know Cordelia and Claudette were estranged and had been for decades."

"For what reason?"

"They were both in love with the same man."

Foley raised a brow. "Ohhhh. That'll do it."

"It seems Claudette knew him first. She fell for him, and then he met Cordelia, and his affection shifted from one sister to the other, according to Claudette."

"Are you referring to Marlon Bennett, or are we talking about a different man?"

"It was Marlon. In Cordelia's first letter, she tried to make amends with her sister. The second letter is much the same except for the ending when Cordelia makes a comment about fearing for her life."

"She give a reason why?"

"She did not, but Claudette believes her sister had seen or overheard something that led to her murder."

"Funny thing to suggest, given they weren't in contact with each other, isn't it? Pure speculation on Claudette's part, if you ask me."

"Maybe not. When Cordelia was younger, she had a hobby of observing people. She'd jot things down that she saw or overheard in a notebook."

"Interesting."

"When you searched the house, did you find any notebooks or journals? Any notes she'd taken anywhere?"

"Nothing, and we were thorough in our search of her place. Looks like she'd given up her childhood habit."

"What about notes she might have typed on a computer or another tech device?"

Foley shook his head. "We didn't find a desktop or a laptop in the house. There was a tablet. It had a handful of eBooks downloaded onto it. Looked like the type of books men would read. My guess is the tablet belonged to Marlon. I took it he preferred reading digital books, while Cordelia preferred physical ones. There are stacks of them all throughout the house. We opened several of the books she had. All of them have book plates on the inside cover in Cordelia's name."

Sounded like Foley may be right: Cordelia had given up the hobby of eavesdropping altogether.

Or maybe she was still doing it, but she no longer wrote down her observations.

I liked the theory about Cordelia seeing or knowing something she shouldn't have. It was a solid motive for murder that made sense to me. What didn't make sense was the fact that Cordelia didn't get out of the house much after Marlon died, making the odds she'd witnessed or overheard something she shouldn't have slim at best.

"Did you hear what I just said?" Foley asked.

"Sorry, I was just running some theories in my mind."

"Care to share?"

"I think we were on the right track the night the murder took place. The attack on Cordelia could have been a targeted one. It's just, if she was a recluse after Marlon died, I don't see her being involved in many situations where she had the chance to see or hear something she shouldn't have."

"Even so, it's a theory I'd like to pursue. So far, I can't figure out how to give it legs, you know?"

"This is why I like the idea of Claudette hiring my agency to look into her sister's murder," I said. "If we work together, sharing our information, I believe we'll uncover what happened to Cordelia, and why, in no time."

He looked at me, saying nothing for a moment.

"Hey, listen," he said. "About my behavior when you first got here. I didn't mean to get snippy with you."

I guessed it was the closest thing I would get to an apology.

"We all have bad days," I said. "I get it. I know I'm not always easy to deal with, but you deal with me anyway."

"I want to talk to you about what's going on. Believe me, I do. You and I, we've always been straight with each other. It's just … I'm not supposed to say anything to anyone."

"Not supposed to say anything about …?"

He breathed out a long sigh. "Your sister."

My sister?

Now I wasn't going anywhere until he told me everything.

"What about Phoebe?" I asked.

Foley and Phoebe had started dating two years before. Given he was the chief of police and was now part of the family had its advantages.

It also had its disadvantages.

When we first met, he hadn't been keen on the two of us working the same investigations. At the time, he'd just been hired as a detective for the county, and the idea of a private investigator coming in and solving a case before he did didn't go over well. Over time, we'd learned to work together, and I was certain his relationship with my sister played a role in it.

"Is there something about Phoebe I should know?" I asked.

He laced his hands behind his head, thinking. "If I tell you, she might kill me."

I shot him a wink. "And I might kill you if you don't."

"If I'm being honest, I've wanted to talk to you about it."

"So talk. If Phoebe gets upset because you did, I'll deal with her."

Another pause and then, "She had a miscarriage, Georgiana."

A miscarriage.

I hung my head.

Of all the things I thought he would say, Phoebe having a miscarriage wasn't one.

"When did it happen?" I asked.

"Last week."

"I didn't even know she was pregnant. I don't think anyone did."

"We were planning on telling everyone once we hit the three-month mark, which would have been next week."

"I'm so sorry."

"Yeah, me too."

"I didn't even know the two of you were trying for a baby."

Phoebe had been married once before, to a man named Jack. He was her high school sweetheart and a man I thought she'd be with for the rest of her life. He'd been murdered four years earlier, shot in the backyard one night while their daughter Lark looked on. She was seven years old at the time.

As the killer was making his exit, he'd spotted Lark staring at him through her bedroom window. Knowing she was a witness to the murder, he abducted her. At the time, I was off grid, mourning my own daughter, who'd died in a tragic pool accident. Prior to her death, I'd worked as a detective for San Luis Obispo County. After, I detached from everyone ... until I learned Lark had been kidnapped. It compelled me to return home to Cambria. Lark's kidnapping had given me purpose and a new lease on life. Not too long after, Lark was found, alive and as well as could be expected at the time. She was eleven now, and after four years of therapy, she was starting to thrive again.

After Jack's death, I worried my sister would never be interested in finding love again. And then Foley came along, showing her that love could be found when you least expected it.

"How is Phoebe doing?" I asked.

"Not good. I hope you don't mind me saying, but she shared something with me about you."

"I'm guessing she told you about my miscarriages."

He nodded. "It's one of the reasons I thought we should talk. You know what she's going through."

"They happened a long time ago, but I still think about it at times. The pain never goes away—not all the way."

"If anyone can get through to her right now, I believe it's you."

"Why hasn't she reached out to me about it?"

"She wants to, but she hesitates because she remembers what it was like for you when it happened. She's afraid if she tells you, you'll relive those memories all over again."

"I've mourned their losses, and I've done what I can to move past them. You were right by telling me, and I appreciate you for it."

He laced his hands behind his head. "What will you do now that you know?"

"I'd like to speak to her. She'll need to know you told me, of course, but Phoebe is an understanding person. If it does upset her, she won't stay that way for long."

"If she's angry at me, we'll get through it. I've tried everything I can think of to support her during this time. She's just so despondent. I don't know what else to do."

"Leave it to me," I said.

He was about to say something more when the office door opened.

Whitlock poked his head in and said, "Mr. Branson is here, and he wants to speak with you. Are you two about finished up with your conversation?"

"Are you referring to Benjamin Branson, the man running against Octavia Bloom for mayor?" I asked.

"I am," Whitlock said. "I assume he's making the rounds.

Although he did press me with questions about Cordelia Bennett's case. He's interested to know how it's coming along."

"So is Octavia," Foley said. "She was here this morning. The two of them are driving me crazy."

"Why?" I asked.

"It seems they're both looking at the murder investigation as something that might bolster their campaigns if they stay involved somehow. They both want their names attached to it. I want them off my back. I don't have time to indulge their personal agendas."

"What do you want me to tell him?" Whitlock asked.

"Show him in. I'll see him ... this once."

Benjamin Branson entered Foley's office, offered him a quick hello, and the two of them shook hands. Foley sat at his desk and offered a chair to Branson, but the man remained standing.

"I won't be long," Benjamin said. "Thank you for taking the time to meet with me, Chief Foley. I know how busy you must be right now. It's much appreciated."

"What can I do for you?"

Benjamin turned toward me like he wondered who I was and why I was in Foley's office. But since Foley hadn't said anything about giving the two men their privacy, I decided to stay. If it turned out he was there because of Cordelia Bennett's case, I wanted in on the conversation.

Benjamin acknowledged me with a nod. "Hello, I don't believe we've met."

"We haven't. I'm Georgiana Germaine. I run Case Closed Detective Agency."

"Ah, yes. I've heard great things about it, and about you."

"And I hear you're running for mayor."

He crossed his arms, beaming with pride. "I sure am."

Benjamin's physique suggested he made the most of his gym

membership, if he had one. He looked to be in his mid-fifties and had a thick head of salt-and-pepper hair. He was dressed a bit more laidback for someone running for mayor, in a short-sleeve Polo shirt and black jeans, but perhaps his visit was a casual one.

"I've been impressed with what Octavia Bloom has done for the county in her time as mayor," I said. "Do you think you can beat her?"

He raised a brow. "I appreciate your honesty, and I agree. Octavia has done a remarkable job. I'd say we both have our strong suits. She brings a certain skillset to the table, and so do I. Different strengths, so to speak."

Spoken like a true politician.

"Octavia went to high school with my mother," I said. "They're good friends."

"Ah, makes sense."

"I'm guessing you're here to talk to me about the Bennett murder," Foley said.

"Correct. It's been a couple of weeks, and I was wondering where you're at in your investigation."

Foley had been right.

Benjamin did appear to be here to further his own agenda.

"Bloom wants the same thing," Foley said. "Now let me tell you what I want and what I don't. I don't want this case to take center stage in either one of your elections. It isn't right, and it doesn't sit well with me."

"I understand."

"Do you? A woman is dead. We have a lot of eyes on us right now. People are concerned, afraid it might happen again if we aren't quick to catch this guy. I'm sure a lot of people who live in the area are thinking if a woman was murdered at the local library, a woman could be murdered anywhere around here. I won't allow Cordelia's death to be turned into a political media circus."

"I agree. All I want is for the murderer to be found and brought to justice so everyone can breathe again, go back to their normal lives where they're not afraid to leave their houses."

"You say all you want is for the killer to be brought to justice, but when all is said and done, I'm guessing you'll want to take some credit, say you had a hand in it somehow, right?"

Benjamin sighed. "I believe you have me all wrong."

"Oh, yeah? How so?"

"How much do you know about my background?"

"Not much."

Foley may not have, but I'd been following Branson's candidacy ever since he announced he was running.

"Your priorities if elected are to make housing more affordable and reduce carbon emissions, and the crime rate in the county," I said.

"Well said," Benjamin said. "Someone's been doing their homework."

"I like what you've had to say about crime in particular. The county has one of the highest crime rates in America. Residents here have a one in twenty-one chance of being targeted for violence or property crime. It needs to change."

"I agree." He shot me a wink. "Maybe I'll get the chance to win your vote after all."

"We'll see."

"I don't mean to interrupt your conversation, but I have other appointments I need to get to today," Foley said.

"Of course," Benjamin said. "Like I said before, I don't want to take up too much of your time. The reason I asked if you knew anything about my background is because I know what it's like to have a loved one murdered. My mother was killed when I was eleven. They never caught the guy who did it."

Foley leaned back, lacing his hands behind his head. "Oh, I didn't know."

I didn't either.

"Did you grow up around here?" I asked.

He shook his head. "I'm from New Orleans."

"What brought you to California?"

Foley shot me an irritated look like he wanted me to move things along. And while I wanted to respect his other appointments, I was enjoying the conversation with Benjamin a little more than I cared to admit.

"I went to college here, Stanford University. Guess I fell in love with the place. Been a resident of the state ever since."

Ever the skeptic, Foley said, "Why do you want to be updated on the investigation, anyway? What is this need for involvement?"

"Let me start off by saying I understand your concern. It would be easy for you to assume I have an agenda to bolster my campaign if my name is associated with it."

"Makes sense, doesn't it? It sure seems to be Octavia's agenda. Because she's a woman and the victim is also a woman, I assume she thinks her involvement would be appealing to female voters."

"Did she say as much when she came to see you?" I asked.

"Not in so many words."

"So, she didn't say it. You assumed it."

Foley huffed an irritated, "My assumptions tend to be right."

Not always, though I wasn't about to mention it, not after hearing about what he and my sister were going through.

"I'm not here for political reasons," Benjamin said. "When it comes to murders like this one, I suppose I have some unresolved issues. And the fact this latest murder has taken place in my own backyard, I'm hoping it won't be too long before its solved."

"We're doing everything we can to make sure we find the person responsible," Foley said. "And we'll be doing it with Georgiana's help."

"Oh?"

"Cordelia Bennett's sister came to see me this morning," I said. "She's hired my agency to conduct our own investigation."

Benjamin clapped his hands together. "This is fantastic news. The two of you working together should speed things up, and then we can all move on."

And there it was—his secondary motive—if it was, in fact, secondary.

With the murder being the talk of the town, it overshadowed the election, putting the late Cordelia Bennett in the spotlight, a place I was sure Benjamin and Octavia had expected they'd be right about now.

Benjamin turned toward Foley. "If you have a few more minutes to spare, would you fill me in on what you know about the case so far?"

Foley and I exchanged glances, and I hesitated, waiting to hear how much he was willing to divulge.

"We're following up on a couple of leads, talking to the neighbors of the deceased, and those who knew her," Foley said.

It was an answer that wasn't an answer, which told me he wanted to exercise caution, keeping the more intimate details close to the vest for now.

The plan suited me just fine.

Foley seemed to have no desire to mention the note we'd found at the library or what was said at the end of one of the letters Cordelia sent her sister. He was offering Benjamin breadcrumbs, and Benjamin struck me as an intelligent man, someone who would pick up on it.

"Any theories yet? Suspects?" Benjamin asked.

"No suspects. As far as we're aware, no one saw the murder

take place. If they have, they haven't come forward. We've taken several items into evidence. Once everything is examined, we hope it will produce new leads. Now, if you'll excuse me, I have a full day of work ahead of me."

Benjamin appeared dismayed with Foley's response, but he was quick to say, "Of course. I won't take up any more of your time."

"I appreciate it."

Benjamin left Foley's office, and I followed suit. Once we reached the hallway, he turned back, looking me in the eye as he said, "I'm thrilled to hear of your involvement with this case. Let's talk again soon."

I nodded, certain we would talk again, sooner rather than later.

Phoebe was dressed in a pair of blue silk pajamas when she greeted me at the door, and her hair was disheveled, like it hadn't been brushed in days. She looked frail, which made me wonder if she'd been eating. She had big, black circles under her eyes and what looked like the remnants of old mascara stuck to her cheeks.

She tipped her head toward the bag I was holding and said, "What's in there?"

"Ben & Jerry's ice cream. I've brought Chewy Gooey Cookie for you and Chocolate Therapy for me. Can I come in?"

She swung the door all the way open and waved me inside. "Sorry, the house is a mess. I gave the cleaners the week off, and I just haven't felt up to doing any housework this week."

To say the house was a mess was an understatement. Unlike me, who couldn't relax at the end of the day unless my home was tidy and in order, Phoebe had always struggled in the cleanliness department.

Today, her house had the distinct aroma of pizza. There were piles of clothes everywhere, some dishes in the sink, and a watery red substance on the tile floor in the kitchen. Given there was a half-empty wineglass on the counter, and an open bottle of merlot next to it, it seemed obvious the watery substance on the floor was wine. If wine was what she needed to cope, I didn't blame her.

Seeing the house in its current state stirred up my anxiety, but I was determined not to let it show, or to dive right in and start tidying the place myself.

Phoebe noticed me looking around and said, "I know, I know. There are clothes everywhere. It's like a clothing bomb went off in here."

"It's all right."

"I was going through our closets last week, removing items we no longer wear and outfits Lark has outgrown. I planned on donating it all. I just need to get everything bagged up so I can drop it all off."

"I have some time. Do you want some help?"

"I'd love some. Are you sure?"

"Tell me where the bags are. I'll load everything up and drop it off for you."

We walked to the kitchen, and she opened one of the cabinets, pulling out a box of plastic bags. I removed the ice cream from the paper sack, setting both pints on the counter.

"It's nice of you to bring ice cream, but I don't think I can eat it right now," she said. "I'm kinda doing a liquid diet, if you know what I mean."

"It's fine. I just ate, so I can wait on having mine too."

I opened the freezer, placing both containers of ice cream inside.

"It's not like me to drink wine in the middle of the day," she said.

"I know it's not. There's no judgment here."

She reached for her wineglass. "Want some?"

Given it was one in the afternoon, and I had a meeting later with Simone and Hunter, I passed. "I'll tell you what, let's share a bottle next time I'm here. Sound good?"

"Sure."

She added more wine to her glass, and we headed to the living room. As soon as she sat down, she said, "I know why you're here. I'm guessing he's told you what happened."

I stared at her for a moment, trying to think of the right words to say.

"Come on, now," she said. "I'm too exhausted to dance around it, Gigi. It's not like you to stop by unannounced with pints of ice cream in the middle of the day."

I sat on the floor next to a pile of clothes and started bagging. "You're right, and yes, I know what happened, and I'm so … sorry."

"When did you find out about the miscarriage?"

"Foley told me this morning. We can talk about it if you want, or we don't have to talk about it at all. It's up to you. I just want you to know I'm here for you, for whatever you need."

"I appreciate it."

"And hey, I hope you're not upset with him for sharing the news with me. As far as I know, I'm the only person he's talked to about it, and even then, I had to pull it out of him. I knew something was wrong the minute I saw him today. He needed to tell someone, to express how he's feeling. I'm glad he told me."

She leaned back, yawning. "I'm not upset with him for sharing it with you. It wasn't fair of me to ask him not to tell anyone. It's something I've been thinking about a lot today. He's been so attentive to me over the last week, waiting on me from the moment he gets home until we go to bed. He's been taking care of Lark, helping her with homework, picking her up from school."

"He's a good guy."

"This morning, I realized I've been so involved in my own

grief, I hadn't stopped to think about what he's going through. *I didn't lose a baby—we both did.*" She took a sip of wine and added, "How did he seem to you when you saw him?"

"A bit irritable, and not like his usual self, but it's to be expected. He's worried about you."

"Lark is too, and I feel so bad about it. The last thing I want is for her to carry the burden of what's happened. She didn't know I was pregnant. No one did. When I had the miscarriage, we thought it was best to tell her, so she'd know why I haven't been acting like myself. Maybe we shouldn't have told her, though. I'm thinking it was a mistake."

"Why?"

"Every morning when we get her up for school, she says she feels unwell, and the truth is, she's fine. I think she's nervous to leave me."

"It's understandable."

"I know. I just sit here thinking about it all day, knowing she's at school and unable to concentrate because her mom is having a meltdown."

"You're doing the best you can, given the circumstances."

"Am I? Because it sure seems like I'm not."

I knotted the top of the bag of clothes and grabbed another bag. "Do you want to talk about it?"

"To you, yes. But it doesn't feel right. I don't want to stir up bad memories."

"I'll relive it either way. Talking about it doesn't make it better or worse. It doesn't change anything. And to be honest, I've made peace with my past ... as much peace as I can, anyway."

She took a deep breath in and said, "I didn't know it was going to be this hard. When you went through it, I thought I knew what you were feeling. I thought I could empathize. I was so wrong. I know that now."

"You were a great support to me," I said.

Phoebe took another sip of wine and walked to the kitchen, pouring herself another helping of merlot. She returned to the living room, setting the glass down on a side table. Then she plopped down on the floor next to me.

"I'm glad you're here. It's made me want to get off my butt and do something for the first time since it happened." She grabbed a bag and a fistful of clothes and joined me in my efforts. "How did you do it? How did you get through the loss of a child—twice?"

"I just took it one—"

She pressed her hands to her face, bursting into tears. "I'm sorry. I thought I could talk about it, but I'm not sure I ... it just hurts too much, you know?"

I dropped the clothes I'd just scooped up and wrapped my arms around her. "You have no reason to be sorry. If you need to cry, cry. If you need to scream, scream. Let it out. Let it all out."

And she did, wailing for the next several minutes, while I sat there, holding her. All the emotions she'd been keeping at bay came flooding out. And though it pained me to see her in such a state, our shared experience allowed me to understand her in a way most could not.

Minutes ticked by, and as the tears subsided, she relaxed enough to revisit the subject once more. "I don't know how to get through what's happened. I've felt pain before, but nothing could have prepared me for losing a child."

"I think the best thing you can do is to be patient with yourself. Take it one day at a time."

She leaned against the sofa and said, "I'm trying."

"Like you, I experienced an anguish I'd never known when it happened. Both miscarriages came before Fallon was born. The only time I've suffered worse was when she too was taken from me."

"Taken from all of us. How did you get past it, to the place you're in now?"

"I didn't for a long time, and then one day, I decided I needed to acknowledge it and to honor the children I'd lost."

"How?"

"With the first, when I learned I was pregnant, I was overjoyed. I went out and shopped for the baby, buying neutral clothes, fitting for a boy or a girl. I bought toys, and bottles, and pacifiers. Then the miscarriage came. For the first few weeks, I tortured myself, spending most of my time in the nursery, surrounded by all the things I'd bought. I even slept in there a few times."

"I had no idea."

"I didn't want anyone to know. I thought it was better that way, but you know something? It wasn't. I should have leaned on the people who cared about me, people I trust. To honor the baby's life, I stuck everything I'd bought for the baby in a box. I dug a hole in the backyard, put the box in the hole, and I had my own private ceremony. It was the healing process I needed. It didn't make everything feel fine again, but it helped."

"It gave you a sense of closure."

"It did," I said.

"I'm not sure I'm there yet."

"It's been a week. You don't need to be there yet. You don't need to move on until you're ready."

"There's so much guilt attached to it all. Not moving on makes me feel like I'm not being a good wife or a good mother."

"It's okay to let your husband and even Lark look after you right now. You should lean on them, and you should lean on us, your family. It's what we do."

She nodded, then said, "Let's talk about something else. Tell me about you. What's going on in your life?"

I wanted to tell her I had set a wedding date, but now didn't seem like the right time. As I considered whether I should or not, I thought of my mother, who'd never been any good at keeping things quiet.

"Giovanni and I have picked a wedding date," I said.

A smile crossed her face, and she reached out, grabbing my hand and giving it a squeeze. "I'm so happy for you both. When's the big day?"

"August of next year."

"Where?"

"We're having the ceremony and the reception in Giovanni's sister's backyard."

"Ooh, at the family estate in New York. Perfect."

"I wasn't sure whether I should talk to you about it or not yet. But Mom knows, and I can't believe she hasn't said anything to you already."

"She's been away at a girls' weekend with her friends. If she wasn't gone, I bet I'd know by now. I'm glad you told me. It's nice to think about something positive to look forward to next year."

I tied a knot in the last bag. "Looks like we're all done here."

"I appreciate your help. Hey, I've been meaning to ask you about Mom's neighbor, the woman who died."

"Cordelia Bennett. Her sister came to see me this morning. She's hired me to investigate the murder. It's the reason I was at Foley's office today."

"It's strange, isn't it? The murder makes no sense to me at all."

"You're over at Mom's place a lot more than I am," I said. "Did you ever meet Cordelia?"

"I talked to her a few times. I always thought she was such a nice lady. Did you know her?"

"I met her once, and I'd see her outside in her garden from time to time, but she never made eye contact with me. From what I know about her, she liked to keep to herself."

Phoebe rolled a rubber band off her wrist, using it to pull her hair up into a loose bun. "If you've taken her case, there's something you should know."

"Go on."

She leaned in like she was getting ready to tell me a secret, even though we were the only two people in the house. "About a month ago, I saw Cordelia arguing with her next-door neighbor."

The fact Phoebe had seen Cordelia arguing with her neighbor was good information. Everything I knew about Cordelia so far led me to believe she avoided people—and thereby, arguments —as much as possible.

"Do you happen to remember the exact day of the argument?" I asked.

"It was the first of October," Phoebe said. "I remember because I'd just gotten my hair cut, and I stopped by Mom's house to take her to lunch."

"Tell me what you saw."

"I'd just pulled into the driveway. Mom said she needed five more minutes before she was ready, so I waited for her in the car. It was such a nice day, I decided to put the window down, and I saw Cordelia open her front door. She walked right over to her neighbor and started talking to her. Everything seemed okay at first, and then the neighbor got angry, and they started arguing."

"Do you know what they were arguing about?"

She shook her head. "I was too far away to hear their conversation."

"Which neighbor?"

"The one in the pink house."

I knew it well.

The pink house, which I'd always referred to as the Pepto Bismol house, had been on the market for some time. The darling older couple who'd owned it had priced it far higher than it should have been. It sat vacant for a while, and then the couple wised up. They reduced the price, but not by much. When it still didn't sell, they reduced it a second time, and then a younger couple swooped in and made an offer, which the owners accepted.

"Have you met the couple who bought the house?" I asked.

"I haven't."

"Mom makes it a point to know everyone in the neighborhood. I'm guessing she's met them. Did you tell Foley about the argument you witnessed?"

"I did. He stopped by and talked to the woman last week."

"Did he tell you anything about their conversation?"

"He said the wife was polite. She remembered speaking to Cordelia, but she denied they'd had an argument."

"Are you sure they were arguing that day?" I asked. "I believe you. I'm just trying to get all the facts straight."

"One hundred percent. I know what I saw."

"Did Foley happen to mention their names to you?"

Phoebe nodded. "The wife's name is Rosalyn Westwood. Can't remember the husband's name."

"Did Rosalyn tell Foley what her conversation with Cordelia was about?"

"She said Cordelia's cat kept getting out, and it was hanging out in Rosalyn's yard, which upset her dog."

"I didn't know Cordelia had a cat."

"It's Mom's cat now."

"What?"

"I guess you haven't been to her house since she took the cat in. Spoils the dang thing more than she ever spoiled us."

We both laughed.

It was good to see her smiling again.

"I never thought Mom was an animal person," I said.

"Me either. Guess she is now."

Maybe Rosalyn was telling the truth, and the argument had been over a cat. Or maybe she was lying, and the story about the cat was a diversion, smoke and mirrors to keep Foley from the truth.

"When you saw them arguing, did it seem like they were discussing a cat?" I asked.

"In my opinion, whatever they were disagreeing about seemed a lot more heated."

"How so?"

"I may not have heard what they said to each other, but the more they talked, the more upset Rosalyn became. At the end, she started pointing at Cordelia's house in such a way that made me think she was telling her to get off her property."

"Did you see how their conversation ended?"

"I did. Cordelia walked back to her place, and she was wiping her eyes. I think she'd started crying. I thought about going over and seeing if she was all right, but I didn't want to get involved. Now I'm wondering if I should have."

"It's hard to know what to do in that situation."

"Their conversation has been on my mind ever since I found out she died. I've been wondering if there's more to the story than what Rosalyn says."

"If there is, I'll find out."

"I know you will."

"I'm glad you told me about this," I said. "Sometimes the smallest detail makes the biggest difference."

"What are your plans with the case?"

"I'm meeting with Simone and Hunter to discuss it. Might be a good idea to have Hunter do a background check on the Westwoods. You never know when it might lead to something."

"It's the reason I thought you should know."

"Cordelia was the type of person who kept to herself. I don't see her getting into a lot of situations where she'd put a target on her back. Because of that, anyone who had interactions with her before she died is suspect to me, including her neighbors." I stood, grabbing the bags we'd filled with clothes and walking them over to the door. "Is there anything else I can do for you before I go?"

She threw her arms around me and said, "The fact you took time out of your day to stop by and check on me is all I needed."

"If there's anything I can do, I want you to call me, any time, day or night."

"You want me to grab your ice cream so you can take it with you?"

"Let's leave it here. I'll stop in tomorrow and see how you're doing. Maybe by then you'll have your appetite back, and we can enjoy a glass of wine and an entire pint."

I was back at the office, sitting on a sofa with Simone and Hunter. Today, Simone was wearing a Pet Shop Boys T-shirt beneath a black blazer. Her curly, black hair was styled into box braids and pulled back into a bun on top of her head. Her look was a sharp contrast to Hunter's long, red pigtails and bohemian-style wide-leg jumpsuit.

Hunter kicked off her moccasins and leaned back on the couch, crossing her legs in front of her. "It's sad. The poor lady lived a long, happy life, save for the loss of her husband, only to have it end in murder."

"I've been hoping we'd be able to get involved in her case," Simone said. "What can you tell us about it?"

Not much.

"Cordelia was shot once in the chest, but once was all it took to kill her," I said. "I found a gun on the ground not far from her body. It was registered to Cordelia, and it wasn't the murder weapon. I'm thinking she knew someone was in the library with her, and she knew she was in danger. She may have been trying to defend herself, but she didn't get the chance before she was shot."

"Do the police have any suspects yet?" Simone asked.

"They don't, and we're still not sure what the motive was, but I believe it was a targeted attack."

"Why?"

"There are a few things I should mention. Whitlock found a note on the floor the night Cordelia died. On it was a physical description—short curly hair, seventies, glasses—which is a perfect description of Cordelia."

"Doesn't seem like a coincidence."

"I don't think so either," I said.

"The killer may have dropped the note and left it behind on accident."

"It's possible, and there's one other thing about the note that I should mention. The note could have been referring to Cordelia, but the description on it also matches the woman who manages the library, Samantha Swan. Samantha was supposed to be closing the library the night of the murder, but Cordelia offered to stay in her place so Samantha could attend her granddaughter's volleyball game."

"Do you think the wrong person was murdered?" Simone asked.

"It's one of the things we need to figure out. If the note is connected to the murder, it could also mean someone was hired to kill Cordelia."

"Ooh, murder for hire. We haven't dealt with that before."

Hunter opened her notebook and began taking notes.

In our murder investigations, Simone and I chased down leads and interviewed people associated with the crime, and Hunter worked behind the scenes, gathering information at the office. She preferred it that way, remaining in the background, by herself, away from people.

"Is there anything else we should know?" Hunter asked.

I stood, walked over to my desk, and grabbed the letters

Claudette had left with me. I returned to the sofa, handing one letter to Hunter and the other to Simone.

"Our client left those with me. As you know, Claudette and Cordelia were sisters. Cordelia sent two letters to her sister before she died," I said. "Hunter, I gave you the first letter. Go ahead and read through it."

She nodded and unfolded the letter, her eyes scanning over it until she was finished. "There was bad blood between the sisters. Did they ever work through their issues before Cordelia died?"

"They did not."

"Do you think it's the reason Claudette hired you?"

"I do. There's an element of guilt, regret there—that they hadn't resolved matters before Cordelia's death."

"Why was there bad blood between them?"

"They were both in love with the same man. In the end, he chose Cordelia, and they got married. Claudette never forgave her for it."

"Talk about sibling rivalry at its finest," Simone said.

"Your letter is similar, Simone," I said. "But there's one big difference."

"I'm intrigued," Simone said. "Let's get right to it,"

She read the letter aloud.

As she neared the end, she gasped, clasping a hand over her mouth.

"What is it?" Hunter asked.

"At the end of this letter, Cordelia says she fears for her life," Simone said. "How long was it between the time Cordelia sent this letter and her death?"

"A few days."

"If someone was planning to murder her, it looks like she had good reason to be concerned," Simone said.

"I saw Phoebe earlier today, and she told me something

interesting," I said. "About a month ago, she was at our mother's house. Cordelia lives across the street. While Phoebe was in the car, waiting for our mother, she saw Cordelia fighting with the next-door neighbor, a woman named Rosalyn Westwood."

"Did she know what the fight was about?"

"She couldn't hear their conversation, but Cordelia was crying at the end of it. When Phoebe found out Cordelia had been murdered, she told Foley about the conversation she'd witnessed. He talked to Rosalyn, and she told him their interaction wasn't a big deal. According to her, they had a disagreement over Cordelia's cat coming into the yard and riling up her dog."

"I don't see how that would lead to murder," Simone said.

"Truth is, Rosalyn could have given any reason for the argument," I said. "As far as I know, no one else witnessed what happened or heard their conversation."

"Do you think Rosalyn could be lying?"

"I'll have a better idea after I speak to her again. I'm going to stop by and see her in the morning."

I heard a strange clicking sound and then all went quiet.

"Hang on a minute," I said. "I'll be right back."

I walked to the kitchen. Popping my head inside, I noticed nothing was on—the refrigerator wasn't running with its usual hum, and the time wasn't displaying on the microwave.

I returned to Simone and Hunter. "Looks like the power is out."

"Hope it won't be for long," Hunter said.

"I guess we'll see," I said. "Where were we?"

"What can we do to help you get things started in the investigation?" Simone asked.

"There's not much to go on so far, but I was thinking we should circle back to the people Cordelia was with right before she died. There are two employees who worked with her at the library, Samatha Swan and Johnny Mansfield. I've spoken once with Samantha, but I haven't talked to Johnny yet. Simone, I'd like you to speak to them both tomorrow."

"Sure thing. Anything in particular you want me to say or ask?"

"If you can, talk to them one on one, not together. Ask them about their relationship with Cordelia. I want to know if she ever mentioned anything to them about fearing for her life, or whether either one of them noticed any changes in her demeanor prior to her death."

"What can I do?" Hunter asked.

"For now, I'd like you to run background checks on Rosalyn Westwood and her husband. It may be irrelevant, but it's a start. By this time tomorrow, I'm hoping we have a direction to go in, and some good leads for tracking down our murderer."

Rosalyn Westwood was dressed in a pair of joggers, an oversized sweater, and a Raiders ballcap when I parked in front of my mother's house. There was another car parked in front of mine, a fancy black Mercedes I didn't recognize.

Rosalyn had just locked the Pepto Bismol house door, and it looked like she was heading out to walk her dog. For a moment, I considered saving the conversation I'd planned to have with her until later. If I waited until she was out of sight, I could sneak around the property while she was away. Then again, just because *she* wasn't home didn't mean her husband wasn't there.

I exited the car, glanced in her direction, and noticed her eyeballing my car. She pivoted and headed in my direction, a wide grin on her face as she said, "Nice Jaguar. What year?"

"It's a '37. It belonged to my grandmother."

"Your grandmother had good taste."

"She did. The car was passed down to me when she died."

"I love classic cars. I've never owned anything else. I've seen this beauty parked here a few times, and I've always admired it. How do you know Darlene?"

"She's my mother."

"Ahh, I see. Which daughter are you?"

"I'm Georgiana, the private detective."

"Thought so. You have a *private eye* look about you."

I wasn't sure what the 'look' of a private eye entailed, but in my vintage, wide-legged linen trousers, black sweater, and matching wedge shoes, it seemed I'd nailed it.

"'I'm guessing you've met my mother," I said.

She smirked at me. "You can't live on this street and not *know* your mother. She'd never allow it."

She laughed, and I followed suit, glad we were off to a good start.

"Your dog is adorable," I said.

"Thanks so much. He's a Morkie."

"A what?"

"A cross between a Maltese and a Yorkshire terrier. His name is Boomer, and today's his birthday. I'm going to get him one of those doggie cupcakes later. Do you have any pets?"

"I have a Samoyed named Luka."

"One of those dogs that looks like a wolf. They're beautiful."

Though I was enjoying our conversation—and the fact I'd been able to establish a rapport without putting in much effort—it was time to segue the light conversation we were having into something heavier.

"It's a shame, what happened to your neighbor," I said.

Rosalyn glanced at Cordelia's house then back at me. "I still can't believe it. She was always so nice to me."

Yeah, but were you always nice to her?

"How well did you know Cordelia?" I asked.

"We talked here and there when we saw each other, but she was on the quiet side. When we did talk, she kept the conversation brief. She seemed sad. I guess it's because her husband died."

"I heard you weren't fond of her cat."

Rosalyn cleared her throat, stunned to find out I'd heard about the conversation she'd had with Cordelia about the cat, *if* it was about a cat.

"How did you know about—"

"My sister is married to the chief of police," I said. "I heard he stopped by to talk to you about an argument you had in your front yard some weeks back."

"I wasn't aware he'd told anyone about our conversation." Rosalyn blushed, fluttering her eyelids. "It wasn't a big deal. I just asked her if she could do a better job at keeping her cat from coming into my yard."

Blushing was her first strike.

Fluttering her eyelids was her second.

Both were telltale signs that she was lying to me.

I considered pointing it out to her, but given we'd just started the main topic of conversation, I decided to wait and see what more I could get out of her first.

"When the conversation between you and Cordelia ended, I hear she started crying," I said.

Rosalyn's eyes darted back and forth.

Strike three.

She was about to be called out.

"I don't ... ahh, I don't remember Cordelia crying," she said. "She was a little upset, sure, but not to the point of shedding tears over it. We had a good conversation. When she left, every-thing was fine between us. I thought it was, at least. What makes you think she was crying?"

"During your conversation, my sister was parked right about where we're standing right now. She witnessed the entire exchange."

Rosalyn pressed a hand to her chest. "Gosh, she must have seen something I didn't then. Maybe Cordelia started crying after I went back inside the house. I had no idea what I said had upset her so much."

She had *some* idea.

Of that, I was certain.

"If my sister said Cordelia was crying, she must have been," I said.

"I ... I don't know what to say."

It might have been the most honest thing she'd said so far. I'd backed her into a corner, something she hadn't seen coming. The only way out was for her to tell the truth, and it was clear she wasn't about to do that.

"Did you have any other conversations with Cordelia before she died?" I asked.

"A couple of small ones, I guess."

"What did you talk about?"

She paused a moment and then said, "I don't recall. Small talk, about the weather, or her garden, or the neighborhood, that kind of thing."

"Did Cordelia ever say anything to you about fearing for her life?"

"What? No. Why would she fear for her life?"

"I don't know."

"Then why did you ask the question?"

Why, indeed.

"Cordelia sent her sister a couple of letters before she died," I said. "In one, she alluded to being afraid, which makes me think she knew something was about to happen to her. And she'd been right—something did happen."

Rosalyn squeezed her eyes shut like she was trying to produce tears, though the tears didn't come. Was it an act? If so, she'd failed.

"Oh, my goodness, I can't believe it," she said. "Poor thing."

I glanced at her wrist. "That's a big greenish-yellow bruise you got there. Based on the color, I'd say it's a couple of weeks old. What happened?"

Rosalyn slapped a hand over the bruise, but it was much too late. In the time we'd been chatting, I'd also noticed a small gash over her left eye. I wondered if she had other gashes and bruises, ones I couldn't see.

"It's nothing," she said. "My shoelace came undone when I was out walking Boomer not too long ago, and I fell. What's with all the questions?"

Her tone had changed a great deal since the start of the conversation. At first, it had been light and warm. Now her tone was low, responses flat.

"What can I say," I said. "I'm a private investigator, and I'm curious about things."

I heard a rustling sound coming from a bush nearby, which didn't make sense, given there wasn't a breeze today. Rosalyn seemed to notice it too, and she turned, both of us staring in that direction.

I squinted, looking closer, but I didn't see anything, and the rustling had stopped.

Rosalyn glanced at Boomer, who was dancing around her feet like he was losing patience. "I should go. So much to do to celebrate his birthday. It was nice meeting you, Georgiana."

It may have been nice, though I expected it wasn't, and given I was sure she'd lied to my face, the feeling wasn't mutual.

"Is your husband at home?" I asked.

"Eddy? No. He's out of town for work. Why?"

"I was hoping to ask him some questions."

"What questions?"

"I'd like to know about his relationship with Cordelia," I said. "When do you expect him back?"

"I don't know."

"*You don't know* when your husband gets off work? Why not?"

"He'll get here when he gets here. And just so you know, he didn't have a relationship of any kind with Cordelia—I doubt they'd even spoken to each other. I don't think he'd be much help to you, but I'll tell him when I see him."

"I'll be talking to everyone in the neighborhood at some point."

"I get what you do for a living, but aren't the police investigating this one?"

"They are. I've been hired by a private individual to do the same. I'll be working alongside the police until we catch the guy ... or girl responsible."

She swallowed, hard, and said, "Oh, well, I wish you the best of luck. See ya."

Forcing a smile, she tugged on her dog's leash. "Come on, Boomer. Let's go."

Beneath her smiley exterior was a woman who seemed to have a lot to hide.

The next time we talked, if she *had* lied to me, I'd find a way to ensure her lies came spilling out.

14

I showed myself inside my mother's house and glanced around, not seeing anyone, but hearing voices coming from the kitchen. I made my way there, expecting to find her with Harvey, and the owner of the Mercedes parked out front.

When I entered the kitchen, my mother looked up at me and said, "Georgiana, how nice of you to stop by."

"How was your girls' weekend?"

"Grand," she said. "We had the time of our lives in Palm Springs. Made a bunch of new friends, to boot. I just wish it wouldn't have gone by as fast as it did."

Sitting next to my mother was a woman I knew but hadn't seen in person in some time.

The woman smiled at me and said, "It's been a while, Georgiana. Nice to see you again."

"And you, Mayor Bloom."

She shot me a wink. "I've known you since the day you were born. It was Octavia then, and it's Octavia now."

"How's the campaign for reelection going?"

"It's going well. Benjamin is a formidable opponent, but I feel confident I'll be voted in as mayor for another term."

"I met Benjamin yesterday. He stopped at the police department to talk to Chief Foley about the case we're working on."

My mother's eyes lit up. "*We*? Am I to believe Claudette took my recommendation, and she came to see you?"

I nodded. "She stopped by the office this morning."

"Claudette's a bit tightly wound, wouldn't you agree?" my mother asked. "And not much in the way of conversation. I got the impression she didn't like me when we met. She took my advice, at least."

"She does get straight to the point. I was surprised when I learned you sent her to me. In the past, you've always been nervous when I'm investigating a homicide."

"I'll be nervous this time as well, I can assure you. It's just ... the more I've been thinking about what happened to Cordelia, the more I realize I want the best for my friend. And the best is you, dear. No offense to Foley or Whitlock. They're decent, I'm sure you'll agree, but they don't have your talent for solving murders."

We all had our talents, and even though I had a spotless track record of solving every case that came my way, it never felt right to take all the credit for myself. It was a team effort, no matter what percentage role we each played.

"Georgiana, would you mind if I asked you a question?" Octavia asked.

"Not at all. What's the question?"

"What did Benjamin want to know about the investigation, if you don't mind discussing it?"

In some ways, I did mind.

Though she was a family friend, Benjamin deserved the same privacy and respect as she did. I tried to think of a way to spin it, to say something without saying too much, a little game of dodge-and-confuse.

"He asked a lot of questions," I said. "Did you know his mother was murdered when he was a child?"

"I know just about everything there is to know about him. I wouldn't be a good opponent if I didn't. We talked about it once. I get the impression it's something he's never gotten past. It's a shame that it's still a cold case."

Eager to get off the subject of Benjamin, I took the conversation in a new direction. "Foley said you stopped in asking about the case as well."

"Yes," Octavia said. "I was hopeful at the start, but my visit wasn't well received. Chief Foley is certain I want to be part of the investigation for political gain."

"I wouldn't say it's your *ulterior* motive."

Octavia tipped her head, blinking up at me. "You think *I* have a motive?"

"If I'm being honest, I believe you and Benjamin both do. You may be running against each other, but I think your motive concerning the homicide investigation are one and the same."

"And what motive would that be?"

"The sooner this case is solved, the sooner both of you will be back in the spotlight, where you want to be, so voters' minds return to the election."

My mother's eyes widened. "Georgiana! I'm surprised at you. How could you say such a thing to such an old friend of mine? If Octavia has a motive, it's no different than every other person's in this county. We all want to see the killer caught and brought to justice."

Octavia swished a hand through the air. "I appreciate your candor, Darlene, and you're right, but so is Georgiana."

"Oh? How so?" my mother asked.

"The murder investigation takes some of the momentum out of the previous plans I'd put into motion. As such, I've had to make some adjustments, which is fine. It happens. I also need to focus on what the residents in the area need right now. There's a good deal of fear and uncertainty surrounding this murder. It will be a relief when we can give everyone peace of mind."

"I agree," I said. "If I were in your position, I'd want the case solved so I could get back into the forefront of voters' minds too. I don't fault you for it."

"I know you don't."

My mother smiled, pleased the topic had been resolved in an amiable way. "Are you able to stay for a few minutes, Georgiana?"

"I have some time, yes."

"Good. Come, sit down and I'll pour you a glass of iced tea."

I took a seat at the table, and while my mother prepared the iced tea, Harvey entered the room.

"Hey there, when did you get here?" he asked.

"A few minutes ago."

"I didn't hear you come in."

"Guess what?" my mother said. "Georgiana has been hired to investigate Cordelia's murder."

Harvey sat in a chair next to me and said, "Is that so? Glad to hear it."

I'd decided to stop by my mother's house to speak to her and Harvey about my conversation with Rosalyn. But given Octavia was there, I hadn't decided whether I should go forward with the discussion or return and speak with them another time.

As I contemplated what to do, Harvey said, "I know you've just started your investigation, but what can you tell us about it? Do the police have any leads yet? I asked Foley about it the other day. He didn't have much to say."

I hesitated, something Octavia seemed to pick up on.

"If you don't want to discuss it in front of me, I can go," she said. "I have plenty of other things to attend to while I'm in town today."

"Guess what," my mother said. "I've been assisting Octavia here and there with her campaign."

Octavia glanced in my direction. "It's true. My assistant's father is going through chemotherapy, and she wanted to be there for him. My husband has been helping me ever since, but then your mother offered to step in, and she's been a great help. It was just supposed to be until I found a replacement, though no one can replace your mother."

"And no one should," my mother said. "Why hire someone else when your best option is ready, willing, and at your disposal? I'm honored, truth be told. Besides, I run circles around those young whippersnappers at your office, too."

"You sure do."

I glanced over at my mother. "Now that we're getting close to the election, will you have to be away more?"

"Oh, no," my mother said. "I'll still be home every night. I just have to make the drive from here to Octavia's office in San Luis Obispo certain days of the week. Much to be done!"

"With you at my side," Octavia said, "I'm sure Benjamin Branson doesn't stand a chance."

My mother blushed, raising a finger. "Flattery will get you everywhere with me ... and you aren't wrong."

Harvey yawned, fisting a hand in front of his mouth. "I do believe it's time for my midmorning nap. Whaddya say, Georgiana? Any part of the case you want to discuss before I lie down?"

Still undecided, I took a deep breath in. "It's important to me that what little details we have aren't made public knowledge until Foley decides the time is right."

Octavia nodded. "Of course. If there's anything you want to say, you have my full discretion."

While I appreciated her words, I made the decision to go with a "less is more" approach.

"Since I was just hired today, we're just getting things going," I said. "We're focusing most on who interacted with Cordelia in the weeks prior to her death."

"I'd say it would be a short list," Harvey said. "She didn't seem to get out much, not that we noticed anyway."

"We're starting by talking to those she worked with at the library. I had a brief conversation with the library manager on the night of the murder, but she was in shock. Simone is following up with her today, as well as another male employee who works at the library."

"Good plan."

"The reason I was in the neighborhood this morning is because Phoebe witnessed an argument about a month ago between Cordelia and Rosalyn."

"Did she now?" my mother asked. "She made no mention of it to me."

"I don't think she thought much of it, not until she heard about what happened to Cordelia."

"What did she see?"

"She was sitting in her car with the window down, but she wasn't close enough to hear what they were saying to each other. When the conversation ended, Cordelia was crying. After hearing Cordelia had died, Phoebe told Foley, and he stopped by and had a chat with Rosalyn."

"What did Rosalyn have to say for herself?"

"She downplayed the whole thing, acting like it wasn't an argument. She said they'd had a talk about Cordelia's cat being in her yard too much, which irritated her dog. Maybe Rosalyn thought Cordelia did it on purpose, though it's not like you can train a cat to pester a neighbor's dog. Cats do what they like, when they like."

"Phooey," my mother said. "Zoey is the sweetest cat I've ever known. Doesn't have a nasty bone in her chubby little body."

"Where is Zoey? I heard you took her in."

My mother returned to the table, setting a glass of iced tea in front of me. "I can't say. She's around here somewhere. She disappears sometimes, but she always comes back when she's hungry or in need of attention."

"I just had a conversation with Rosalyn in the front yard," I said. "It was strange."

"In what way?" my mother asked.

"She says she doesn't recall seeing Cordelia crying that day."

"And do you believe her?"

"I don't."

"Why not?"

"I asked her several basic questions about the conversation she had with Cordelia, and I could tell she was lying to me."

Octavia crossed one leg over the other, leaning closer. "What makes you think she was lying?"

"Georgiana can spot a liar a million miles away," my mother said. "Her precious father was the same way. If she says Rosalyn is lying, she must be."

"What I don't know is *why* she lied to me," I said. "Maybe it's because we've just met, and she doesn't know me. I get the impression there's more to it, though. Mom, have you talked to her much since she bought the house?"

"Oh yes, we've spoken on several occasions. I've always found her to be a kind woman. A bit standoffish, but kind, unlike that rotten husband of hers."

"I asked if he was home, and Rosalyn told me he was out of town for work."

My mother rolled her eyes. "Doesn't surprise me. Eddy's been in and out ever since they bought the place."

"I take it you don't like him."

"Not one bit. Every time I engage him in conversation, he shuts me down. I have no idea why. I've shown them nothing but kindness since they bought the place. Ask me, he's not a people person, and he has no interest in having anything to do with his neighbors. Cordelia was the same in that respect."

"Did she ever say anything about Eddy?"

"Oh, let's see now. Guess it would have been right after the couple moved in. She brought over a loaf of bread she'd baked. And you know, it wasn't an easy thing for her to do. She wasn't a people person, as you know, but she still did it. Eddy almost slammed the door in her face before his wife turned up. Who does that? I'll tell you who. A man with no manners."

"Did you ever see Eddy mistreat Rosalyn?"

My mom swished a hand through the air. "Nah. Like he would do it in front of my face. Believe me, if I had seen anything, I wouldn't have stood for it, as you well know. He would have had an earful from me."

"When was the last time you saw him?"

My mother leaned back, tapping a finger against the chair, thinking. "Let's see now ... it would have been before my girls' trip. Wait, no. Now that I'm thinking about it, I suppose I haven't seen him for some time now, not since Cordelia died."

Harvey nodded, adding, "You know, neither have I."

My mother had a spare key to Cordelia's house, a key she'd given me on the night of Cordelia's murder. When Cordelia and Marlon were still alive, they liked to go on cruises. While they were gone, my mother would feed the cat, water their plants, and keep an eye on things.

Foley and Whitlock had confirmed they'd done a thorough search of the house. Any evidence they deemed relevant to the case had been taken. And given it wasn't where the murder had taken place, it wasn't a crime scene. I didn't feel an ounce of guilt about going inside and looking around.

When I entered the house, I found it to be in order. Whatever had been disturbed when the police searched the premises looked like it had been put back to its original location. I guessed it was Whitlock's doing. The two of us had bonded over many things as we'd worked together, cleanliness being one of them.

The first thing to catch my eye was the photo wall Claudette had told me about. She was right. It was filled with pictures of the two sisters, distant memories from a happier time. As I looked at each photo, I realized they had been arranged in chronological order, from the time they were kids until, what I guessed to be the last photo I guessed they'd taken together before their relationship imploded.

It was nice to see the sisters in earlier times, happier times where the two of them posed arm in arm for the camera, without so much as a worry between them. At least that's the story the pictures told. Whether there was any truth to it remained a mystery.

I thought of Phoebe, and how much light she brought into my life. I couldn't imagine a life without her in it. Thinking of her now, I took out my cell phone and sent her a text message, checking in with the hope she was doing better today than yesterday.

I stuck the phone back in my pocket and shifted my focus to the master bedroom. It was straight down the hallway at the end. I made my way there and flipped on the light.

The bed was made, the decorative pillows in perfect order. On the floor was a pair of red slippers, and on the nightstand, a dainty woman's bracelet. A poetry book rested next to it—*The Love Poems of Lord Byron*. A bookmark inserted into it showed it was halfway read.

I grabbed the book and opened it, reading the inscription on the inside:

To Cordelia,
The love of my life.
My days are full of an unexplainable bliss, and it's all because
of you.
All my love, Marlon

I flipped through the poems, and then set the poetry book back where I'd found it.

It felt strange being here, like I was an intruder, roaming

around inside a place I didn't belong, each room like a time capsule, gathering dust. And yet, it still had life, buzzing and vibrating from the tick of the clock on the wall to the sound the heater made as it kicked on. It gave me the feeling Cordelia might walk in the door any moment, even though she never would. She'd been laid to rest now, ashes to ashes, as they say.

I turned my attention to the right side of the room and the three oversized windows. The blinds on each were drawn. I walked to the one in the middle, turned the wand, and as the blind opened, I looked out.

I was shocked to see I had a perfect view into the West-woods' living room. Their black, sheer curtains were halfway closed, but even so, I imagined with a little light, Cordelia would have been able to see right through them.

Had Cordelia stood where I was standing now, snooping through her neighbors' window to pass the time?

If she had, what had she seen and overheard?

I shifted my focus to the windowsill.

A pen rested on it.

I picked it up, noticing it was almost out of ink.

I closed the blinds and continued looking around the room. Nothing caught my eye. Nothing of significance, anyway. I moved through the house, opening drawers and cabinets, hoping to hit the jackpot, to find she'd left behind a series of journals, a note, or a clue, anything to explain why she'd been murdered.

The drawers and cabinets revealed no such thing. If she *had* left such items behind, there was no doubt the police would have found them already. From what I'd been told, their search of the house was a bust. They'd found nothing of interest.

I entered the sitting room, which looked a lot more like a dedicated library than a room one would sit and relax in. Except for a large rug and a curio cabinet, the room was devoid of furniture and had been outfitted with bookshelves. The shelves contained so many books, there wasn't a single empty space among them.

Serious book lovers with tidy library rooms tended to arrange books in a variety of ways, including:

Alphabetically.
Stacked.
By genre.
By height.
By author.
By color.

Upon closer inspection, Cordelia had first organized the books by genre, then by author, from A to Z. She preferred mysteries overall, with the genre accounting for over half the books in her library. The remaining books were a combination of classics, nonfiction, memoirs of famous people in history, a little poetry, and a handful of books on knitting.

Given I didn't have anywhere pressing to be, I decided to pull some of the books off the shelves, just to see if there was anything inside them. I made my way from left to right, pulling out a stack of books and flipping through them before placing them back where they belonged. I did so with precision, though I supposed it didn't matter.

Marlon was dead.

Cordelia was dead.

And I didn't get the impression Claudette shared the same passion for books that her sister had.

An hour passed, and I was beginning to regret my decision.

I'd found nothing of significance, and I'd just started on the mound of mysteries, which I estimated might take another two hours to flip through.

I considered stopping, but I was no quitter, so I pressed on.

I'd gone through all the authors with A and B surnames and had just started on the C's when I noticed just how many of them there were. This was due in part to all the Agatha Christie books in her possession. Several of the titles had more than one copy, which confused me at first. Then I looked a bit closer, noticing the duplicate copies weren't the same. They were different editions, published in different years.

A couple dozen books later, I opened a copy of Agatha Christie's *The Pale Horse*. To my surprise, a few pieces of folded notebook paper slipped out, fluttering to the floor. I leaned down, grabbing the pages. The first thing I noticed was that in the center of the top of each page, it said:

From the Desk of Cordelia Bennett

I then noticed the pages had been numbered. I stacked them together in order and began reading.

JUNE 4, 2024

Argument 7:20 p.m.
Glass decoration is thrown, it shatters against wall and
breaks, she cries 7:25 p.m.

JUNE 18, 2024

Yelling, I cannot hear what's being said 9:25 p.m.
She takes a shower 10:05 p.m.
They kiss and fall asleep 10:51 p.m.

JULY 24, 2024

Did someone scream??? 1:51 a.m.
I waited, but it's dark, I can't see anyone 1:55 a.m.
All quiet again 1:58 a.m.

AUGUST 21, 2024

Fighting 9:10 p.m.
He says, "You can't leave. I won't let you leave." 9:12 p.m.
He's crying 9:18 p.m.
She's crying 9:18 p.m.
They make up, go to bed 10:34 p.m.

SEPTEMBER 5, 2024

She's crying, holding her cheek … is she hurt??? 6:47 p.m.
He leaves room, returns with an ice pack, she applies to face
6:54 p.m.
They sit together on the bed, watch TV, everything seems fine
now 8:55 p.m.

SEPTEMBER 29, 2024

He's packing a bag 10:41 p.m.
She's crying, taking things out of it 10:51 p.m.
He's angry, putting things back in bag again 10:53 p.m.
He slaps her, she's hurt, but how badly??? 10:55 p.m.
They walk out of the room 10:56 p.m.
He's yelling, I can hear his voice, but can't see anyone 10:58 p.m.
I hear a truck, and I go to living room window and look out, I
see him pull out of the driveway 10:59 p.m.
He's gone, I think 11:02 p.m.
(Should I go over?? Should I talk to her???)

Is she hurt??? Yes, she's hurt, but I'm not sure what happened.
Did he hit her??? I'm not sure what to do 11:03 p.m.
He hasn't returned home 12:30 a.m.
He still hasn't returned home 2.30 a.m.
I don't know if he's coming back 6:45 a.m

OCTOBER 1, 2024

He's back home 7:21 a.m.

OCTOBER 3, 2024

She's packing a bag, he's not home … is she leaving???
8:02 a.m.
She's crying, zips up one suitcase, takes it somewhere
8:08 a.m.
(Should I go talk to her???)
More packing 8:15 a.m.
I hear a truck, he's home … did he forget something???
8:19 a.m.
She looks scared, grabs bags, trying to find a place to hide
them maybe. Hides one bag, comes back for the other.
8:19 a.m.
He's in the room, he sees the second bag, flips it open 8:20 a.m.
They fight, he hits her, and then he turns, squinting like he's
looking at me
Does he see me???
Does he know I saw what he's done???
She needs help, I must help her, MUST HELP HER
GET AWAY

"We need to talk," I said.

Rosalyn placed a hand on her hip and sighed. "All I want is to have a calm, peaceful day with my dog on his birthday. I understand what you're trying to do, and I'm sure you're questioning all of Cordelia's neighbors, but I don't have anything else to say."

"Are you sure? Because I think you do. I was just taking a look around Cordelia's house, and I found something interesting, something I'd like to show you. Can I come in?"

"Why do you want to talk to *me* about what you found?"

"I believe it might be of interest to you."

"Why? I didn't know her. Not well, I mean. It's sad that she's dead, but I don't see how anything you could show me would be of interest."

"You might, if you hear me out."

Rosalyn ran a hand through the long strands of her straight brown hair and rolled her eyes. "All right. I guess you can come in but make it quick."

I nodded and followed her to the living room.

"Is your husband home?" I asked.

"No, why?"

"I'd like to speak to him. Have either you or your husband ever seen Cordelia peering into your house from her bedroom window?" I asked.

Rosalyn raised a brow. "Peering through ... what?"

I stood a moment, assessing her tone of voice as well as her body language. She was twitchy and unstill. And while it seemed like she was unnerved by what I'd just said, she was avoiding eye contact, so it was hard to tell for certain.

"I found a book in Cordelia's library," I said.

"I heard she owned hundreds of them."

"She did, and I've just been through them all."

"Why would you go through every single one of her books?"

I sat in a chair, crossing one leg over the other. "Seems crazy, right? You might want to sit down for what I'm about to say next."

She shrugged. "I'm good where I'm at."

Where she was *at* was across the room, leaning against the wall, holding the doggo in her arms.

"Before I tell you what I found, I'm going to share something Cordelia's sister told me when we met yesterday to discuss her case," I said.

Another shrug. "Okay."

"Cordelia was a people watcher."

"What do you mean?"

"When they were younger, Claudette said her sister used to take notes about things she saw and heard around town."

Rosalyn's eyes dropped to the floor. She chewed on her lower lip and then pet her dog. Without looking up, she asked, "Why would she do that?"

"I don't know. I guess she was a curious person. Since this was something Cordelia did many years ago, Claudette wasn't sure whether her sister had continued doing it throughout her life. They hadn't spoken in a long time."

"I'm guessing this has to do with the reason you're here?"

"It does. Inside one of Cordelia's books, I found a few pages of notebook paper. She'd written some detailed notes. Based on those notes, it looks like she hadn't given up on her habit of people watching and documenting what she witnessed."

"How do you know the notes aren't old, like from before, when she was younger? If they were tucked away in a book, anything she wrote could have been written a long time ago."

"The notes had dates."

She peered up at me. "Dates? From when?"

"They're from this year," I said. "The first entry on the page was written in June, and the last entry was a few weeks ago. I'd like to read a few of them to you, if you don't mind."

"Can you just give them to me? I can read them for myself."

"I'd rather not," I said.

I proceeded to go over the highlights of Cordelia's notes. At the end, I drove it home with the final words, where Cordelia thought she'd been caught spying. And that she wondered if she could help the woman ... help her get away.

When I finished, I folded the notebook pages, tucking them into my bag. Then I glanced at Rosalyn to gauge her reaction. Her eyes were watery, like she was fighting off the urge to cry, but she didn't.

She walked over to where I was sitting, sinking into the chair across from me.

"Whoever Cordelia was spying on, she felt bad for what she'd seen," I said. "She also felt the urge to help the woman, which makes me wonder if she ever got the chance."

"The woman she was talking about could be anyone."

"I'd be inclined to believe you if Cordelia had gotten out of the house more often, but based on the entry dates, the notes were taken after her husband died. And from what I've heard, Cordelia was so distraught over his death, she didn't leave the house often. It was only when my mother pushed her to take the volunteer position at the library that she started getting out more."

"So, she did get out. Maybe she overheard or saw something that concerned her at the library."

It made sense why she'd suggest such a thing. When I'd read the notes to her, I skipped around and hadn't shared much more than the highlights.

"If you think about how Cordelia set the scene, I don't believe it's possible for what she witnessed to have taken place in a library—or a public place, for that matter," I said.

"Why not? Is there something you're not telling me?"

"I didn't read all the notes to you. In truth, I debated whether I should share them with you or anyone else before they're handed off to the police."

"Then why did you?"

"When I was in her house, I realized Cordelia had a perfect view from her bedroom window into your house."

"I'll bet she had just as good of a view of her neighbors who live on the other side."

The neighbors on the other side.

Why hadn't I thought of that?

I'd been so focused on the woman in the notes being Rosalyn, I hadn't thought to check the windows on the opposite side of the bedroom to check whether Cordelia could see into her other neighbor's house too.

"Is there a reason Cordelia would have spied on one of the neighbors who live on the other side?" I asked.

"Have you talked to them?"

"Not yet."

She shook her head, disappointed. "Well, maybe you should before you come over here insinuating the notes are about us."

"Are you suggesting they *aren't* about you?"

"I am. I don't know much about the neighbors a couple of doors down, but I heard they're getting a divorce."

"Since when?"

"I don't know. They're still living together in the same house, though. I saw them together yesterday, and I haven't seen anyone move out."

"How did they seem?"

"All right, I guess." She went silent for a moment. "Are you married?"

"I'm marrying for a second time next year."

"Then you're aware that no marriage is perfect."

"I am."

"What was written on those notes of hers ... it could have been opinion rather than fact. Either way, it wasn't about us."

She was looking at the floor, again avoiding eye contact.

If she had something to hide, not looking me in the eye was smart on her part, even though it increased my overall suspicions.

"Do you expect your husband to be back today, or tomorrow, or this week?" I asked.

"He's out of town for business. I'm not sure when he's going to be back."

"Don't the two of you communicate about his work schedule? I feel like most people know when their partner is coming and going."

"Eddy's job is complicated. He works in shifts. Sometimes his jobs go short, sometimes they go long. Sometimes he walks through the door without even talking to me first. It's his way of surprising me, I guess."

Was it a good surprise or a bad one?

"I don't know how you do it," I said.

"Don't know how I do what?"

"Handle his crazy schedule. I don't think I could do it."

"I've gotten used to it."

"How long have the two of you been married?"

"It will be two years in December."

"Not long then. I imagine you two must still be in the honey-moon phase."

"I suppose it still feels that way at times."

"Are you from around here?" I asked.

She shook her head. "I'd never been to Cambria before we bought this house."

"What caused you two to settle here?"

"My husband used to come here a lot with his family when he was a child, back when his grandmother was still alive. She lived here all her life. He has fond memories of those times, and he always wanted to have a home here one day. So here we are."

"I hope he considered where you wanted to be before a decision was made. Are you happy living in Cambria?"

She narrowed her eyes like she didn't understand why I cared about her happiness. It gave me the impression she wasn't used to others taking her feelings into account.

"I'm happy enough," she said.

"It's good of you to care about your husband's hopes and dreams. You just don't seem enthusiastic about being here. Am I right?"

Rosalyn set Boomer on the floor, and he scampered off to the kitchen, making a beeline for his water bowl. "I haven't lived here long enough to know what I think about it yet. For a small town, Cambria is all right. Maybe it's not the place I thought we'd end up, but there is a quaint sense of community here. People are nice. It's the reason I decided it was worth giving it a try."

"Did you know Eddy wanted to move here before you married?"

"I guess not, no."

"Seems like that would be something he'd want to discuss. Why do you think he never mentioned it, given his family memories here and all?"

"He was working for another company at the time, and he wouldn't have been able to relocate, so there was no point talking about it. He quit that job and found a new one, and his boss said he'd be fine with us living here if my husband didn't mind traveling for work."

"How far is the commute?" I asked.

"To San Luis Obispo and some of the surrounding areas."

"What does your husband do for a job?"

"He's an environmental scientist."

"I have no idea what one does in that position."

"He collects samples from different areas, things like soil, water, and food, and then they're analyzed."

"Who is his employer?"

"Eco Earth."

She turned, looking out the window.

I was losing her.

"I need to give Boomer a bath," she said. "So, if we're done here ..."

"Sure, thanks for taking the time to talk to me."

We were done, finished with the conversation ... for today.

But it wouldn't be long before we spoke again.

There wasn't a clear view from Cordelia's house into her other neighbor's home, not from the bedroom, anyway. The living room, however, offered a different angle. From there I was able to see into the bedroom, but the view wasn't as good as the one from Cordelia's bedroom into Eddy and Rosalyn's room.

Still, what if Rosalyn was right?

What if I'd pointed my finger in the wrong direction?

I needed to know for sure.

I didn't know much about the neighbors in the white house. My mother had once mentioned that the wife was an energetic, spirited woman, while the husband was plainer than a stale piece of bread—her words, not mine. The wife was outgoing, active in the community. The husband kept to himself, preferring to stay indoors, curled up with a good book or in front of the television.

I locked Cordelia's front door, and I walked next door, pausing when a strange sensation came over me, a sensation of being watched. I turned, canvassing the neighborhood. I saw nothing and no one, but the feeling didn't pass.

I knocked on the door, and a short, petite woman answered,

offering me a wide smile. She looked to be in her thirties and was dressed in pink from head to toe, including the glittery headband atop her head.

She batted her eyelashes a few times and said, "Hi! You're Georgiana, Darlene's daughter, aren't you?"

"I am. How did you know?"

"Your mother and I chat every now and then. She loves talking about her kids. We've had lunch a few times, and she's shown me photos of y'all. She's a proud mom, to be sure."

"Have you lived here long?"

"A few years now. It's a fun neighborhood, lots of cookouts and block parties."

"Do you attend many of them?"

"I try. Most times, I have to go by myself. It's one of the reasons why I appreciate your mom. She always makes me feel included, like I'm not alone."

"Don't you have anyone to go with you to these neighborhood get-togethers?"

"I'm more of an extrovert, while my husband is more of an introvert. Well ... my soon-to-be ex-husband, I should say."

She huffed a nervous laugh and went quiet.

"Soon to be ex-husband?" I asked. "Are you two getting divorced?"

"Sad to say, but yes."

"Why?"

She circled her finger around, pointing at me. "Well, aren't you a curious one? Your mother said as much about you."

I wondered what else my mother had said.

"I don't mean to pry into your life," I said.

"Oh, not at all. I'm an open book, and I've had so many conversations with your mother about you, I feel like I know you."

Terrific.

The subject of oversharing was a conversation I'd had with my mother on many occasions, asking her to respect the fact that I liked to keep my private life private. Privacy was a gray area for her, an area she tried to respect, but oftentimes, she ended up blurring the lines.

I was feeling bothered by the fact a woman I knew almost nothing about seemed to know a lot more about me, details I wouldn't want her to know about. Then again, it was clear she was a Chatty Cathy, which gave me an advantage.

"It's too bad you and your husband can't make your relationship work," I said. "Where did things go wrong?"

She gave the question some thought. "It's difficult to pinpoint. A lot of little things started adding up until they became much bigger things. We're so different. I like to get out of the house and meet new people. I like getting involved in the community. He likes being at home, where it's quiet, so he can snuggle up on the couch with our two cats."

"I may not know you, but from what you've told me so far, it seems like you have a healthy attitude about getting divorced."

"It's been a long time coming, and it is sad. We have a great time together. When I'm at home, and we're just hanging out, we enjoy each other's company. It's just not a lifestyle I want to live day after day. I want someone who will go do things with me. I'm tired of going it alone."

"Does your husband know how you feel?"

She nodded. "He's known for a while. It's just ... I feel stifled. I stay home too much because I know it's what he wants and needs. I wish he'd agreed to go out with me from time to time, but I feel like he wouldn't be happy if he did."

"It sounds like you still feel a great deal of love for him."

"I do."

"Are you sure a compromise can't be reached between the two of you?"

A Siamese cat attempted to slink between her legs and escape out the front door. She bent down and picked it up. "And just where do you think you're going, Major Whiskerton? Nowhere, that's where."

Major Whiskerton?

The name was a bit strange, but I gave her points for creativity.

"I need to put Mr. Whiskerton here in the bedroom," she said. "You want to come in for a minute?"

"I do."

She turned and pointed to the left. "Kitchen's that way. I'll meet you there in a few shakes."

I walked to the kitchen. While I waited, I looked around, noticing most of the windows in my vantage point were open, making the house a lot cooler than I would have liked. Maybe it was what she preferred, a crisp chill in her household air.

The home was spotless. Not a single item in my line of sight was out of place. As far as decorations went, other than plants, there wasn't much to see. And the house had a pleasant aroma of vanilla, which I attributed to a candle I saw burning in the living room.

I stepped into the room for a moment, peering out the window at Cordelia's house. I'd left Cordelia's blinds open and the lights on, but I couldn't see much. Given Cordelia's house was at a higher elevation than both her neighbors' homes, it made sense that she could see things they could not.

"Georgiana? Where have you gone?"

"Sorry, I was in the living room, admiring your plants," I said.

I turned, joining her in the kitchen.

"I'm sorry, I forgot to introduce myself before," she said. "I'm Kayla Collins, and my husband's name is Seth. As to the question you asked before my naughty cat tried to make a run for it, the crazy thing is, I think my husband and I will be a lot happier as friends than we ever were as marriage partners."

It was the most responsible, healthy attitude I'd ever heard from someone going through a divorce. I suspected many, many people remained in relationships when they knew they weren't right for each other for a myriad of reasons, Many people stayed, even when the marriage and the partnership between them was over.

"What does your husband do for work?" I asked.

"He's a yoga instructor."

"Teaching yoga is a job that would require him to work around people, so he must like at least a little bit of social interaction."

"He's been doing yoga since high school. It calms his nerves. It's the one thing he realized he could do out in public that doesn't give him social anxiety, so he got certified, and now he teaches. He loves it. The place he works at is lowkey and has a chill vibe. It's the perfect place for him."

Though we'd never met, I'd started forming a picture in my mind of what I thought he'd be like.

"I guess I should tell you why I stopped by," I said.

"I guess you should, although I bet I already know, since I'm aware of what you do for a career and all."

"I'm sure you've heard all about what happened to your neighbor, Cordelia Bennett, and the murder at the local library."

"We heard. Our heart breaks for her. We just hope the killer is caught soon so she can move on in peace. I imagine her soul won't rest until the man who killed her is brought to justice."

I found her comment curious.

I, myself, didn't know if I believed in such things as spirits not being able to cross over to the great beyond, or wherever it was people went when their time was up. Even so, the idea of being able to offer someone peace through justice put a smile on my face.

"I've been hired to investigate Cordelia's homicide," I said.

Kayla's eyes widened. "Oh? I didn't know."

"It just happened. Cordelia's sister is in town, and she's not interested in the investigation being drawn out any longer than it needs to be."

"Makes sense. I'd want the same thing for my sister."

"I was hoping I could ask you a few questions about Cordelia, since you and Seth were her neighbors."

"You betcha. I'd be glad to help in any way I can, and I expect Seth will feel the same way. Before you knocked on the door, I was just about ready to make a salad for lunch. I have plenty to make two salads. Would you like one?"

"I appreciate it, but I have lunch plans a bit later today. Why don't you go ahead and make your salad while we talk?"

I took a seat at the kitchen table, and she opened the refrigerator, pulling out a variety of veggies and a handful of other items. She grabbed a bowl out of the cabinet and started throwing everything in.

"How well did you know Cordelia?" I asked.

"Not super well. When we saw each other, I was polite, and she was polite in turn. She was ... how do I say this ... a bit standoffish. And you know what's crazy? I'm the extrovert, but she talked to my husband more than she talked to me."

The revelation was unexpected.

"I got the impression Seth avoids people whenever he can," I said. "Maybe I was wrong."

"Oh, no. You're right on every possible level. Except, he recognizes a fellow introvert when he sees one. Kindred spirits, as they say. They both liked to read, and when she learned that about him, they struck up a conversation with him one day, and then she started loaning him some of her books."

"Did he ever talk to you about her?"

"Not much. He's never been a big conversationalist, though. He keeps a lot of his feelings close to the vest."

"It must be difficult for you," I said.

"It can be."

Kayla had been outgoing and spirited from the moment we met, but now I was starting to see a different side of her, a somber side. I had no doubt she'd married for love, and maybe Seth had too. But her needs had never been met, and the day had come when she couldn't lie to herself anymore. I wondered if part of her outlook and optimism with the divorce was a front or a façade to mask the true pain she was feeling.

"When you said Cordelia was a bit standoffish, you aren't the only one who felt that way about her," I said. "It doesn't seem like she allowed many people into her inner circle."

"Your mother was as inner circle as it gets."

"My mother has never seen a challenge she wasn't willing to accept. When it came to Cordelia, I'll bet she pushed her way into her life, whether Cordelia wanted her to or not."

Kayla drizzled some Italian dressing over her salad and laughed. "Your mother does have a way with people. It's a quality few of us have, not to the degree she does, anyway."

I supposed I was like my mother when it came to persistence, except we excelled at it in different ways. I'd always considered myself an introvert, but when push came to shove, I shoved when the need arose.

"I don't have many leads to go on so far in the case, but I did come across something this morning that could mean something," I said.

"Oh? What is it?"

"I was looking through Cordelia's novels. In one of them, she'd stashed a few pieces of notebook paper. She'd written notes, which I believe were about one of her neighbors."

Kayla grabbed a fork, stuck it into her salad bowl, and then she walked over to the table and sat down next to me. "What did she write in the notes?"

"It seems she may have been spying on one of her neighbors for some time, either Rosalyn and Eddy Westwood or you and your husband, I'm not sure which."

"How can you be sure it's one of us?"

"Because of the way she described what she saw. The notes were taken over a five-month period, and they describe a husband and wife who weren't getting along. There's even mention of physical abuse."

Kayla pressed a hand to her chest. "I can't believe Cordelia would have been the type of person to spy on her neighbors. But if she was, I can assure you, Seth and I would have been a snore. *Boring.*"

"In what way?"

"In every way. At home, we're not excitable people, I'm afraid. We're more of a dine together, watch television, read books in bed kind of people."

Nothing Kayla had said so far made me question whether she was being honest or not. And yet, there was a nervousness about her now that I did not detect prior to telling her about the notes I'd found.

It was easy to assume Kayla and her husband were getting a divorce under amiable circumstances. But were they as amiable as she had led me to believe? Or was she a good actor?

"What can you tell me about your other neighbors, Rosalyn and Eddy?" I asked.

She stabbed at a bit of salad with her fork. "I haven't had the chance to get to know them on a personal level, so I can't tell you anything. They seem nice, always give me a wave when we see each other in the front yard."

"Have you ever witnessed anything off between them, any

arguments or spats? Has there ever been anything that would make you question whether their relationship was on the rocky side?"

"I haven't. Like I said, as far as couples go, we don't have a relationship with them. I suppose I've been feeling bad about it."

"Why?"

"I used to be the first one to welcome someone to the neighborhood. But I've been so caught up in my own life for a while, I haven't had the energy to put time or effort into anyone else. Why? Is everything all right between them?"

"I'm not sure. I'd like to speak to Eddy, but he works random shifts at his job. I asked Rosalyn when he'd be back home. She said she didn't know. I find it a little suspicious, living together with someone but not knowing their schedule. It doesn't make sense to me."

"I agree, it's strange. I may not have the perfect marriage, but we always talk about our plans for the day. I can't imagine a relationship where a couple doesn't communicate those things."

I couldn't either.

But just because it was foreign to us didn't mean it was foreign to them.

She went on. "You said Cordelia's notes talked about abuse. What kind of abuse? Physical, or verbal, or both, or ...?"

"As much as I'd like to share more details with you, I don't think I should say anything else until I've had the chance to discuss it with the police department. I hope you understand."

"Yes, of course."

I was about to ask another question when I heard the sound of the front door opening. A moment later, a man entered the kitchen. He had a rolled-up yoga mat slung over his shoulder. He looked unnerved to find someone he didn't know in his home, and he turned toward Kayla, a concerned look on his face as he said, "Who is *she*? And what's she doing in *our* house?"

18

"My name is Georgiana Germaine," I said. "Are you Seth?"

"I am," he said. "Why are you here?"

"I stopped by to talk to both of you about—"

"Why. Are. You. Here?"

He was fidgeting, running his fingers up and down his pants like a nervous tic. Looking at him now, at how agitated he seemed, it didn't seem normal. It crossed my mind there might be some mental issues at play.

If I was right, I wanted to exercise caution. I didn't want to push him or put him in a position where he felt more heightened than he already was in this moment.

Kayla offered him a sympathetic smile and said, "Georgiana is here to talk to us about Cordelia Bennett, honey."

"Why? How does she know Cordelia? And why does she care about what happened to her? Was she a friend? Because I've never seen her at Cordelia's house before."

"My mother is one of your neighbors," I said.

"Who is your mother?"

"Darlene Kennison. She's married to Harvey."

"Good man, good man. But your mother ..." He shook his

head. "Your mother, she's ... don't mind my bluntness, but I find your mother to be a ridiculous, dramatic woman. I try to avoid her."

"I don't mind. I think she's a lot sometimes too. She's a good person. If you got to know her, you'd see that."

"I'm not sure I agree. I still don't understand why you're here, asking about our neighbor. What's it to you?"

"She's a detective," Kayla said. "A private eye."

He turned toward me, blinked a few times, and then said, "Yes, I knew you looked familiar. I've seen you in the paper and on TV in the past. You used to work as a detective for the county. Why'd you quit?"

"I wanted to start my own detective agency."

"You still quit, which makes you a quitter."

Kayla looked my way, mouthing a silent, *I'm sorry*.

"After Harvey stepped down as chief of police, the man who took his position was someone I didn't trust. We didn't work well together, and you're right, I quit. Not too long after, I discovered he had a dark secret, and he'd been murdering people to cover it up."

"I remember," Seth said. "They got rid of that guy, and Rex Foley is the chief of police now, which makes him your brother-in-law. Seems like a decent man."

"He is a decent man," I said.

"If he's so decent, why don't you go back to work for the county?"

It was interesting being on the opposite side of an interrogation.

I wasn't sure I liked it.

"I like having my own detective agency," I said. "Speaking of which, I've been questioning some of Cordelia's neighbors. Her sister hired me to investigate what happened to her."

He was pacing the room now, his hands still running up and down his legs.

My attempt at explaining things in a calm manner had failed.

"Cordelia was keeping an eye on one of her neighbors before she died," Kayla said. "She kept notes, and Georgiana found them."

"I don't understand," Seth said. "Cordelia wouldn't do such a thing—spy."

"Well, she did," Kayla said. "She must have been able to see into one or both of our homes somehow, and she wrote down some of the things she saw. Georgiana was just telling me about it."

"What did she see?" Seth asked.

"The couple wrote about wasn't getting along, and there was mention of possible abuse."

While I appreciated Kayla's desire to help explain the situation, she wasn't making things better. She was making them worse—a lot worse.

Seth glared at me, a nasty look on his face. "Abuse? Is that why you're here? Do you think Cordelia was talking about us? Do you think I abuse my wife? Because I don't, and I never have."

"I haven't formed any conclusions," I said. "I'm just trying to gather information."

It wasn't the *complete* truth.

I was forming conclusions with each conversation I had.

But there was also some truth to what I'd said, and I hoped it was enough for him to believe I wasn't accusing him of anything—yet.

Based on the way he was staring me down, he hadn't believed a word I'd said. He didn't know me, didn't know my intentions. In a way, I didn't blame him for his behavior.

"I want you to leave," he said.

Not unexpected.

In truth, I was surprised I'd lasted as long as I had.

Kayla walked over to Seth, placing her hands on his shoulders. She offered him a gentle smile and said, "Honey, she's just doing her job. She's trying to help, to find out what happened to Cordelia and who would do such a thing to her. We owe it to Cordelia to help Georgiana in any way we can."

It was the best thing she'd said since he'd gotten home, and I paused, waiting for his reaction.

He shrugged her arms away. "We don't owe anyone anything. This is *our* life, and our relationship with Cordelia is no one else's business but our own. Nothing will change the facts, and the fact is ... she's dead. Even if the murder is solved, she's still dead."

In a last attempt to simmer the fire brewing within him, I switched subjects. "I heard you and Cordelia shared a love for books."

"I don't see how our fondness for books has any relevance to your investigation. I want you to leave. I want you to leave now. And don't you *ever* come around here harassing me or my wife again."

Epic.

Fail.

I nodded and said the only thing I could say. "I wasn't trying to harass anyone, and I understand."

"Do you? Because I just asked you to leave, and you haven't moved one inch."

"Wait, Seth," Kayla said. "I know situations like this make you nervous. I promise you, Georgiana is trying to do right by Cordelia. She may be dead like you say, but don't you think her spirit is struggling because her murder hasn't been solved?"

He huffed a nervous laugh. "I don't believe in all of that phooey, and you know it, Kayla."

Silence passed for a moment, and the two of them stood there, staring at each other. I knew now that there was no pulling up from the situation I was in. He'd been angry since the moment he'd seen me in his kitchen. I was strange, foreign, someone he didn't know or trust, and he had no interest in building trust either.

The time had come for me to do what was best for him—to get out of there—

and so I did just that.

"You found these notebook pages inside of a mystery novel?" Foley asked.

"I did," I said.

He scratched his bald head. "I can't believe it. I can't believe you found potential evidence in the one place we didn't look during our search of the house. How'd you get in? Or do I even want to know?"

"If you're worried I busted a window or something, I didn't. I have a key."

"Where'd you get it?"

"My, umm ... my mother gave it to me."

Foley sighed. "I should have known."

"While I would love to take credit for stumbling upon the notes myself, it was the comments her sister had made that piqued my interest. I figured I'd look inside a few of the books, and that turned into looking inside all of them."

"I still can't believe you found what you did."

"Given Cordelia was a bit of a nosey person in her younger years, I was banking on the fact she was still spying on people."

Foley pointed at the notebook pages and said, "Aside from

these, no other notes were found to suggest she'd been keeping an eye on anyone else over the years, right?"

"Right. Maybe she stopped keeping tabs on people during her marriage to Marlon. When he died, I expect she was bored, looking for a distraction, and her old hobby fit the bill."

"You looked through every single book?"

"I did. I hit a point where I almost stopped, and I told myself I was wasting my time. At that point, I'd flipped through most of the books, so I made the decision to keep on going. I'm glad I did. If her murder is connected to these notes, they're our best lead so far."

Foley patted me on the shoulder. "Well done, Georgiana."

Whitlock, who'd been leaning against the wall listening to our conversation, perked up. "I can't say I'm surprised. It's like I've always said—you have talent for this stuff. Always have."

"After reading through Cordelia's notes, what are we thinking?" Foley asked.

"The way I see it, one of the neighbors knew she was having a little look-see into their lives. Maybe she threatened to go to the police. Maybe she confronted them, told them she knew about their dirty laundry, and she was prepared to air it."

"Makes sense."

"If physical abuse is involved, it seems to me someone may have wanted to shut her up before she had a chance to speak her truth," I said. "I questioned both neighbors who live on opposite sides of her. I tried speaking with them, anyway."

"Define *tried*."

"I had a conversation with both wives. Rosalyn's husband was at work, and when Kayla's husband came home and saw me there, he didn't want anything to do with me."

"Why not?"

"I'm not sure. I got the impression he may have mental

health issues, though I hesitate to suggest it. I'd feel awful if I'm wrong."

Foley tapped a pencil to the edge of his desk. "What did the wives have to say?"

"Before I go over those conversations, I want to set the scene and tell you what I could see from inside Cordelia's house. The view into each neighbor's home is different. From Cordelia's bedroom window, I had a perfect view into Rosalyn and Eddy's bedroom."

"What about Kayla's?"

"There's no view from the bedroom, but through one of the living room windows, I had a somewhat obscured glimpse inside Kayla and Seth's house. If I had binoculars, it would be an even better view."

"I see," Foley said.

"Rosalyn and Kayla both said the notes Cordelia took weren't about them."

"Denial, eh? It's to be expected, don't you think?"

"I do."

"The first person I spoke to was Rosalyn. I talked to her earlier this morning, before my discovery, and then a second time after. During both conversations, she seemed nervous, but she strikes me as a nervous person in general. Whether she has something to hide, I don't know. All I can say for sure is my gut is telling me she does."

"What did she say to you?"

"It wasn't so much what she said as what she *didn't* say. I asked her when her husband would be home from work, and she said she didn't know."

"Why not?"

"He works odd days and odd hours, I guess."

"Doing what?"

"He's an environmental scientist for a company called Eco Earth."

Foley jotted down the name of the company. "Never heard of it."

"If someone came to my house with notes suggesting they'd been staring at me through their window and had witnessed possible abuse, I'd involve Giovanni right away. Rosalyn could have picked up the phone, sent her husband a text message or given him a call, and she didn't."

"Good point," Whitlock said. "Or maybe she was waiting for you to leave first."

"Either they have a lack of communication in their relationship, or she didn't want you to know when he'd be home," Foley said. "If it's the latter, the question is ... *why?*"

"Maybe Rosalyn is being abused, and she's afraid to speak up about it. I did notice a bruise on her wrist and a cut over her left eye. Anyway, at the end of our conversation, she pointed a finger at Kayla and Seth, and she mentioned they're going through a divorce."

"We're aware," Foley said. "We talked to every person who lives on that street the morning after the murder."

"So you met Eddy, Rosalyn's husband?"

Foley looked at Whitlock.

"Well, no," Whitlock said. "I was the one to talk to Rosalyn. The husband wasn't home, and I took down a note to circle back with them later so I could speak with him. I haven't gotten around to it yet."

Foley quirked a brow at Whitlock. "The point is, none of Cordelia's neighbors had much of anything to say, nothing that gave us a good enough reason to follow up ... until now. Talk to me about your visit with Kayla."

"Kayla was easy to talk to, and she seemed open to answering any questions I had," I said. "She seemed transparent, and I didn't get the impression she was trying to hide something from me."

"Did she say anything about the divorce?"

"She did."

"What reason did she give for it?"

"She said they're not compatible."

"In what way?"

"He's a homebody who doesn't care much to be around people. She's the opposite. She likes to get out, get involved, change things up instead of enduring the same monotonous routine day after day."

"It's the same thing she told me," Whitlock said. "When she spoke of the divorce, she teared up a few times. It seems it wasn't an easy decision."

"It doesn't fit the usual reasons people get a divorce," Foley said.

"I agree," I said. "She still loves him, I can tell. Even though they're splitting up, she has compassion for him. I witnessed it when he came home. She speaks to him like he's a wounded bird, and she's his safe place."

"She *was* his safe place," Foley said. "I don't imagine she will be once they're divorced. You said he didn't want anything to do with you. Any idea why?"

"He wasn't thrilled to find me in their house, and from that moment on, he was agitated. He was running his hands along his pantlegs, pacing the room. He didn't entertain any conversation about Cordelia. All he wanted was for me to leave."

"What makes you think the husband has mental health issues?"

"The way he acted when I was there wasn't normal. It was irrational, if anything. I'm the last person who should diagnose anyone, but I'll just say it was a feeling I had when I witnessed his behavior."

"How did the conversation end?"

"I didn't want to upset him any more than I already had, and he'd asked me to leave more than once, so I did."

Foley reached for the cup of coffee sitting on his desk, took a sip and winced, like it had gone cold. He set it down, rejecting it.

"After speaking to both couples, what are your takeaways?" he asked.

"I haven't had enough time to process everything they said to me yet. I'm thinking they both need a follow-up visit with someone who has a little more finesse than I do at times."

"What are you suggesting?"

"Whitlock should speak to both wives again, and to their husbands. Afterward, we can reconvene and share notes. Between us, I think we might have a better chance of figuring out if one of them is hiding something."

Foley paused, as if giving the suggestion some thought. "I like it. I like it a lot."

"I like it too," Whitlock said. "I think they've been through enough for one day, so I'll stop in and see them tomorrow. Maybe, just maybe, between the four of them, we'll find some answers."

20

"She won't talk to me," Simone said.

"Who won't talk to you?" I asked.

Simone breathed a long sigh into the phone. "Samantha. From what I understand, she's not talking to anyone. She spoke to the police, but only because she had no choice. She hasn't left the house since the night of the murder."

"Why not?"

"I don't have much in the way of answers. Her husband, Mack, met me at the door. He said his wife wasn't up to seeing me and that she's been freaked out ever since Cordelia was murdered. He's been trying to talk her into seeing a therapist, but she's not interested."

The night of the murder when Whitlock and I had a discussion with Samantha, she'd been overwhelmed by the news, which was normal at the time. I didn't get the impression, however, that she would be affected in the way that Simone was suggesting.

"I'll try and talk to her," I said.

"Since she spoke to you before, maybe she'll be a lot more receptive to you."

"What about the other employee who works at the library—Johnny? Did you speak to him?"

"I did."

"And?"

"He's weird, Georgiana. I couldn't get a good read on him. On the one hand, you have Samantha, who's been acting paranoid since the murder. On the other, you have Johnny, whose attitude about it all is blasé."

"In what way?"

"In *every* way."

"Tell me about him," I said.

"He's skinny, but in an unhealthy-looking way. He talked so fast, it was hard for me to understand what he was saying, not that he was saying anything important. He was rambling, going from one topic to another. Eyes and hands and shoulders going all different directions. I got the impression he was on drugs of some kind when we talked."

"Hmm. What were some of the questions and answers?"

"Not much to tell you there. I asked him about his relationship with Cordelia. He said they didn't have one. When I tried following up with more questions, he kept changing the subject."

"Where does he live?"

"Wildwood Condominiums. And get this—the guy is a feline fanatic. I counted at least six cats during my visit, and I'm sure there were more."

"Sounds like I better follow up with him as well."

"Sorry I don't have anything better to report."

"Don't be. You tried, and that's all you can do."

"How's your day been going?"

I told her about my visits with Cordelia's neighbors and about the notes I'd found.

When I finished, she said, "Wow, I can't believe it. You have amazing luck. You always have."

"Not luck, skill." I winked, and she laughed.

"Noted," she said. "So, what are you thinking now, about the case in general?"

"I want to believe there's a connection between one of Cordelia's neighbors and her murder. Now, I just need to prove it."

21

I sat on the back deck, with a blanket draped over my shoulders, and a glass of pinot noir in hand. As I listened to the sound of ocean waves crashing onto the rocks below, I reminisced about everything I knew about the case so far. The note Whitlock found the night of the murder had been on my mind a lot tonight.

Was it connected to the murder or was I pulling a connection out of thin air because I wanted to believe it meant something when it didn't?

And why was Samantha acting so strange?

Was it paranoia or grief over Cordelia's death?

Or was it something else?

Per my usual at the start of most of my cases, I was left with far more questions than answers. After reading through the dated entries Cordelia had tucked within the pages of the book, I'd started to form new theories. Perhaps one of her neighbors was being abused, as she'd suggested. Perhaps she'd gathered up enough courage to confront the man or the woman or both. If one of them thought there was a chance she'd tell someone else, and they wanted to keep her quiet, it was the perfect motive for murder.

I thought about my earlier conversations with the neighbors. Rosalyn had tried to point a finger at Kayla, and Kayla seemed confused about it all. But was she?

As for either Seth or Eddy being an abuser, Seth was a slender individual, but he was fit, which suited his profession. I didn't know what Eddy looked like, and I also knew nothing of his demeanor, except for what I'd been told. When I'd glanced around their house, I didn't see any photos of the couple anywhere. There had been a collage on one of the walls, but every photo was of their dog.

Giovanni stepped outside, giving my thoughts a brief reprieve.

"Does your wine need to be topped up?" he asked.

I looked up at him and smiled. "I've been so caught up in what happened today, I haven't even had more than a few sips from the first glass you gave me." I lifted the wineglass in the air and shook it. "Still working on it."

He nodded, turned back toward the kitchen, and whistled. Luka, our Samoyed, came trotting outside and nestled across my feet.

Giovanni sat down next to me and wrapped his hand around mine. "Do you feel like discussing your day?"

I did, and for the next several minutes, I did just that. Hearing myself talk about it out loud was therapeutic, and it helped me to piece things together.

When I reached the end, he said, "Of all the people you've spoken to so far, if you had to point the finger at one person right now, who would it be?"

"I don't even feel I can make that call yet."

"Oh, I'd be willing to bet you've leaned on someone as your prime suspect, haven't you?"

He knew me all too well.

"I keep thinking about Eddy, which doesn't seem right, given I haven't even met the guy yet," I said.

"Why him?"

"I have no reason to believe the notes Cordelia took weren't real, which means, someone she was keeping an eye on was getting abused. Seth may have been a jerk to me today, but I don't see him as the type of guy who'd hit Kayla. I could be wrong though."

"Did Rosalyn show any signs of abuse?"

"I noticed a bruise on one of her wrists and a gash over one of her eyes. She told me her shoelace had come undone, causing her to trip. Most of her body was covered up, so I'm not sure if what I saw was the extent of it, or if there was more."

"Did the bruise look fresh?"

I shook my head. "I'd say it was at least a couple of weeks old. Let's say she wasn't lying to me about how she'd sustained the injuries. She still lied to me about other things. Some of her facial expressions were obvious tells. Her eyes would dart back and forth at times when we were talking. And during a few of my questions, she'd flutter her eyelashes—clear tells."

He crossed one leg over the other and leaned back in the chair. "If you had to solve the murder tonight, what would you say the motive was for her murder?"

"I'd say Cordelia was keeping tabs on her neighbors, and she either outed herself or she got caught doing it, and she was murdered because of it."

"It's the most obvious reason."

"Almost *too* obvious. It feels too easy."

"What if it's not? What if you're overthinking it?"

Anyone other than Giovanni wouldn't have gotten away with the suggestion, but he was right. Oftentimes, I overthought everything.

"Let's say one of the neighbors killed her, and let's say it was Eddy," I said. "Why would he go to the library to murder Cordelia when he could have just broken into her house and killed her there?"

"It's never a good idea to murder someone too close to home."

Point taken.

"If Eddy knew Cordelia was going to be working alone in the library, he could have snuck in, waited until everyone left, and then killed her as she was locking up for the night," I said. "Or he could have been following her, waiting for the right moment to present itself."

"Sounds like a decent plan."

"It does, except for one thing."

Giovanni turned toward me. "What's that?"

"The note Whitlock found in the library was a description of a woman. If Eddy had murdered Cordelia, or one of the other neighbors did it, they wouldn't be carrying a note with her description on it. They already knew what she looked like."

"Unless Eddy hired someone to do his dirty work for him."

Another option I'd considered.

Perhaps he'd been lying low until everything blew over and he was sure suspicion wasn't on him. Maybe Rosalyn even knew what he'd done, and she was nervous because she was covering for him. Her story about not knowing when he would return home could have been just that—a story.

Giovanni's cell phone buzzed. He glanced at the screen and then held the phone to his ear. "Yes, Nico, what is it?"

Nico was Giovanni's cousin and worked security at our front gate. As he began talking, I downed the last of the wine and walked to the kitchen for a refill. I'd just stepped inside when I heard Giovanni coming up behind me. He asked Nico to hold on and said to me, "A man just pulled up to our driveway, and he's asking to speak with you."

"What man?" I asked

"I'm not sure. He refuses to give his name or to speak to anyone but you." Giovanni turned the phone toward me. "Take a look. Do you know this guy?"

I leaned over, glancing at the live feed from our security camera. "I know him. Tell Nico I'm on my way."

22

I wrapped a blanket around myself, opened the front door, and made my way down to the street. Nico turned toward me, and I waved, giving him the *all clear* to open the front gate.

I reached the end of the driveway, looked at the man sitting inside the car, and hollered, "Seth, what are you doing here?"

He left the motor running, exited the vehicle, and walked over to me. He didn't say anything at first, so I stood there, giving him a chance to speak before I did. Behind me, I heard footsteps, and I turned to see Giovanni making his way toward us. He stopped to chat with Nico, but I knew he was there to keep an eye on Seth.

Seth still hadn't said a word, and since awkward silences weren't my cup of tea, I broke the silence for him. "Seth, is there something you want to talk to me about?"

"I'm ... there is, yeah. I know it's late. I thought about waiting until morning, but I knew I wouldn't get any sleep tonight if I didn't come over and talk to you. So here I am, okay? I mean, I hope it's okay. Is it okay?"

I wasn't sure what to make of everything he'd just said, so I kept it simple. "It's all right. I know what it's like when something is on your mind. If you're like me, it's better to deal with it sooner than later."

He shoved his hands inside his pockets, kicking a few loose pieces of asphalt and nodding. "I came over to say ... you know ... to say I'm sorry about what happened earlier today. I'm sorry for the way I treated you."

"Please don't take this as me making assumptions, but did Kayla send you to talk to me tonight?"

"In a way. We had a long conversation, and she suggested I make things right. It was my decision to drive over."

The coastal air sent a chill through me, and I pulled the blanket tighter around my shoulders. "Do you want to talk inside?"

He glanced up at the house. "I'd rather not. Can we just talk here?"

"We can ... it's just a bit cold out tonight."

"I understand. I won't keep you long."

He went quiet again.

Maybe he'd said everything he'd come to say, but I suspected there was more, or he wouldn't have still been standing there.

"Is there anything else you want to talk about?" I asked.

"I ... yeah. Cordelia was my friend, and I don't have many friends—not good ones."

You don't say.

"Did you spend much time with her?" I asked.

"Oh, I stopped in here and there after Marlon died, to see if she was doing all right and if she needed anything."

"How did she seem when you saw her?"

"Sad, depressed, quiet. She made a comment once about not having anything left to live for, and it worried me. It's the reason I started visiting more often."

"Did you worry she might take her own life?"

"Nah. She was too savvy of a woman to do anything extreme

like that, but some days I got the impression she was checked out, not listening to me when I was talking. I'm not suggesting she was rude. I think she had a lot on her mind."

"Are you saying she had more on her mind than the loss of her husband?"

He considered the question. "I guess I am. She mentioned her sister to me once. She said she wrote her a letter, and her sister didn't write back. With Marlon gone, it was even more important for her to mend their relationship. She didn't believe her sister would have any interest in patching things up, though, and as far as I'm concerned, she was right."

As unfeeling as Claudette seemed when we met, I wondered if she would have had a change of heart if there had been more time to consider it—time she'd never get back now.

"When you spoke to Kayla, did she tell you about the conversation we had earlier today?" I asked.

"She did, and now that she's explained it to me and I have all the details, I want you to know that I have never laid a hand on my wife."

And there it was, the main reason he'd driven over. To convince me of his innocence.

"I'm not sure what to think about the notes Cordelia took," I said.

"Well, those people she was talking about ... they weren't us. I can't imagine she'd spy on a friend. I don't believe she would have done that to me."

No one wanted to believe it, and yet, I didn't get the impression that any of Cordelia's neighbors knew the *real* Cordelia— perhaps not even my mother.

"Kayla told me you two are going through a divorce," I said.

"We are. Wish things could be different between us. She's the best thing that's ever happened to me. Can't imagine life without her." Seth shook his head and sighed. "Sorry. I've said too much."

"It's fine to speak your mind. Kayla had a lot of nice things to say about you when we talked. I can tell she still cares for you. I'll ask you the same thing I asked her. Do you think there's any way you could work things out instead of getting a divorce?"

His eyes darted around—to me, to Giovanni, to Nico—then back to me. "She's given me so many chances, more than I deserve. I want to step up, to be the man she needs. Every time I try to be that person, I fail. I can't imagine her moving on and being with anyone else, but I think she'd be a lot happier."

"Are you saying you're okay to let go of what you have together because you think someone else could make her happier than you do?"

"When you say it like that, it doesn't sound good, does it?"

"No, it doesn't."

"I don't know. I don't think I'm capable of ever being the man she needs."

"I know we've just met, but Kayla seems like a wonderful woman, and a reasonable one," I said.

"Oh, yes. She is the best person I know."

"Then why not at least consider fighting for her and for your marriage?"

He hung his head, muttering, "This isn't what I came here to talk about. I'm uncomfortable talking about it."

"I understand, but maybe it's something you *should* be talking about with someone. Sometimes it's good to be uncomfortable. Discomfort has a way of bringing change at times, helping us see things within ourselves we wouldn't have seen any other way."

"Huh, I suppose you have a point."

"On the exterior, Kayla seems happy and outgoing. But I

sensed something else while I was talking to her, something beneath it all."

"Like what?"

"There's a sadness within her, and I think it has to do with the divorce. I'm not convinced she wants it. I think she's confused."

"Yeah, maybe."

It looked like he was overwhelmed, so I left it there. "Anyway, I've said my peace. I hope you at least think about things."

He offered me a weak smile and then turned, heading for his car. When he reached it, he opened the door and glanced back at me. "There's one more thing."

"What is it?"

"I know something."

"You *know* something?"

"What I mean to say is, Cordelia shared something with me."

"What's that?"

"One afternoon after I got home from work, I stopped in to return a book she'd loaned me. She gave me another, and we had a brief chat. Before I left, she said she wanted to ask me a question."

"What was the question?"

"She said it was hypothetical, but I'll admit, I've given it a lot of thought in the last two weeks."

I leaned in a little closer, waiting for the juicy nugget I hoped was to come.

"She asked me what I would do if someone I knew was in trouble," he said.

"What did you say?"

"I said it would depend on what kind of trouble they were in, and if it was any of my business to interfere. People are always getting involved in other people's business, giving unsolicited opinions, that kind of thing. I want no part of it."

I wondered if a smidgen of what he'd just said was a dig toward me for inserting my opinions about his marriage into our conversation.

If it was, it was well played.

"Did Cordelia tell you what kind of trouble the person was in?" I asked.

"She didn't. I asked, and she seemed nervous, and she didn't want to keep talking. As I was leaving her house, I tried once more to get her to open up. It didn't work. She said she shouldn't have brought it up in the first place. It was her own burden to bear. She didn't want to get anyone else involved."

"Any chance you remember when the conversation took place?"

He nodded. "It was a few weeks before she died."

23

I woke to find myself in a bed that was unfamiliar, and it wasn't mine. The bedside lamp was still on, and as I sat up, my eyes came to rest on a handmade patchwork quilt.

Where am I?

And how did I get here?

I moved the quilt to the side and stood, noticing I was still dressed in the same pajamas I'd put on before I'd retired to bed. Tiptoeing to the bedroom door, I pulled it open. It creaked as I did so, and I poked my head out, peering into the hallway.

I saw no one at first.

But I heard a sound—humming.

I followed the noise to a sitting room filled with books. A woman was inside, sitting in front of an antique wooden desk. She was hunched over it, writing. As her face came into view, everything became clear.

I was in Cordelia's house.

And I was dreaming.

I approached Cordelia's desk and tapped her on the shoulder. "Excuse me, can we talk?"

She swished a hand through the air. "Not now. Come back later."

"I can't. It isn't how it works."

She huffed a hearty sigh and set the pen on top of the paper. "I suppose if it must be now, I can spare a few minutes. What's on your mind?"

"You're writing a letter."

"I am."

"To whom?"

"I'd like to say it's to my sister, though she'll never receive it, not this one."

"Then why write it?"

"It occurs to me my soul is not at rest. I should have driven to her house when I had the chance. I should have forced her to see me. I didn't because I don't have the backbone she's always had. So I decided to write one last letter, for my own peace of mind."

"What's in the letter?" I asked.

Cordelia smiled and said, "I'm telling her everything I would have said had I worked up the nerve to see her face to face."

"What do you hope the letter will achieve now?"

"I believe it will allow me to move on and not be stuck here, in a purgatory of sorts. I'm ready to be rid of this place, to be reunited with Marlon. The sooner, the better."

"So you know you're ... that you are ..."

"Spit it out, dear. I'm dead."

"You were murdered in the library. Do you know who killed you?"

"If I gave you the answers you seek, it would take all the fun out of you figuring it out for yourself, now wouldn't it?"

I supposed it was the reason my questions were never answered in dreams of this kind, and I doubted they ever would be.

"Have you any suspects?" she asked.

"I've started questioning people. Do you have any advice for me?"

"Advice can be tricky once you've left one place for another. Let me see ... I suppose I don't have any advice. I was scared, you know, at the end. It's true what they say about your life flashing before you before you die. Except my visions were of every fond memory Marlon and I ever shared together. It was beautiful, and it alleviated my fear."

"Why were you keeping an eye on your neighbors before you died?"

"Someone needs to look out for those who can't look out for themselves."

"Are you referring to Rosalyn or Kayla?"

"You tell me. Was it Rosalyn, or Kayla, or someone else—someone you haven't considered yet?"

"Did you see something you shouldn't have? Is it the reason you're dead?"

"I've seen lots of things in my day. I guess I got a little tired of it in the end—sitting back, doing nothing. It's what's wrong with society, and I played a part. We see things, and we turn away because we think we're weak. We think we're better off letting someone else step in or not doing a single thing. It wasn't right of me, not right at all."

"What did you see, Cordelia? What secrets were you hiding?"

She turned away from me, yawning as she said, "You're keeping me, you know. Keeping me from my Marlon. You don't need my help to find the answers you seek. Trust yourself. You'll find your way."

"Wait, please. Can I have a minute, just one more minute?"

As the words left my lips, she started to fade.

"Don't go," I said. "Not yet."

"I must. I'll leave you with this ... Things aren't black or white. People have a reason for the choices they make sometimes. You'd do well to remember that."

24

The following morning, I was sitting on the couch at work, filling Simone and Hunter in on the evening I'd had. When I got to the part about Seth, I realized how much I wanted to believe he was a good person—a troubled person, but a good one. I wanted to believe Seth and Kayla were *both* good people.

But was it clouding my judgment?

Part of what Seth had said to me the previous night was so precise, it almost sounded scripted, like he'd memorized it. I'd spent the morning creating a scenario in my head of what might have happened once I left their house. Kayla had told him about our conversation, what we'd talked about before he'd arrived home. Once Seth learned Cordelia may have witnessed a handful of uncomfortable interactions between him and Kayla, they formed a plan to make me believe they were innocent. A plan that removed all suspicion from them and put it on ... well, anyone else, as long as they weren't the focal point.

A scenario, at least.

Seth wanted me to believe Cordelia was his friend, which was a bit odd, but not so odd that it was unbelievable. He'd claimed he checked in on her on multiple occasions. They chatted about books. He asked if there was anything she needed. And most of all, right before she died, she almost confided in him.

I couldn't decide whether his story was the full truth, a partial truth, or not much of the truth at all. There was no one to back it up, except his wife. A wife who could have been protecting him as well as herself. She was the protective type.

"Hey, Georgiana, come in ... over," Simone said with a laugh, snapping her fingers in front of my face. "Wherever you are, you're no longer here with us."

"I'm sorry," I said. "Seth's visit last night has been weighing on my mind. I'm not sure what I think about it. My head and my heart, or should I say, my emotions are at odds."

"You're suspicious by nature," Simone said. "It makes sense."

"Being suspicious is a good thing," Hunter added. "It's how you solve cases."

"It never feels good when I find out a person I see as a suspect is innocent."

Hunter shrugged. "It's part of the job, isn't it?"

It was part of the job—one of the tougher parts.

As I thought about the day ahead, the office door opened, and an unwanted visitor strolled in, looking smug and full of himself. I wondered if he'd noticed the eyeroll I'd just sent his way. If he had, he'd ignored it.

He flashed me a big smile and walked over.

"Hello, ladies, I'm sorry to interrupt."

"Simone and Hunter," I said, "This is—"

"Benjamin Branson," Simone said. "You're running for mayor."

"I am."

He held out a hand. Simone shook it. Hunter did not, recoiling back onto the couch like she wanted to melt into it.

Turning toward me, he said, "Georgiana, I need a few minutes of your time ... *if* you don't mind."

I did mind.

I minded a lot.

"Why?" I asked. "If you're here to try and get information out of me about the case, you wasted a trip. Until I have something more concrete, there's not much more to say that you don't know already."

"Are you sure?" he teased. "From what I hear, you made a big find yesterday."

Was he baiting me?

Or did he know something he shouldn't?

If so ... *how* had he come by the information?

"How would you know about what happened yesterday?" I asked.

Sensing the irritation in my voice, Hunter and Simone stood, exiting the room and ducking inside the kitchen.

Benjamin grinned, seeming all too happy to have them out of the way.

"You didn't answer my question," I said.

"As to knowing what you found, I have my sources."

"Do your *sources* have names?"

"The source does have a name."

I had to admit, I was intrigued.

"I assume your source isn't Foley or Whitlock, because they wouldn't share confidential details about the—"

"Let me stop you there. The information did not come from them. We haven't spoken again since our meeting in Foley's office."

Why was he bugging *me* for information, then?

Why not go to them?

Perhaps he saw me as the easier target. A gross lack of good judgment on his part.

"I cannot imagine who else would give you information you shouldn't have," I said.

"Why does it matter so much to you?"

"Why does it matter so much to *you*? Why aren't you focusing your time on your campaign?"

He threw his hands in the air. "What can I say? I'm a great multitasker."

"I'm trying to conduct a clean investigation, one without leaks. When a leak gets out into the public before it's supposed to, it compromises what we're trying to achieve."

"I have the utmost respect for your process, believe me."

"Do you? Because you still haven't given me the name of your source."

"His name shouldn't matter."

His name.

We were getting somewhere, at long last.

"His name matters a lot," I said. "You have a choice to make. Give me the name, or I have nothing further to say."

"That would be a shame. I'd hoped we'd be able to work together on cases like these once I become mayor ... for the good of the community, of course."

"Assuming you become mayor."

Benjamin took a seat and crossed one leg over the other. "Has anyone ever told you that you drive a hard bargain? You should have been a lawyer. I bet you wouldn't have lost a single case."

"I was the captain of my debate team in high school," I said.

He shook his head. "Figures."

"As for my cases, I'm well suited to life as a private investigator. I feel like we keep veering off the topic at hand. If you won't reveal your source, I'd like you to leave."

It had been some time since I'd had a good verbal sparring

session, and I found myself enjoying it far more than I should have.

Benjamin flattened a hand and raised it, as if suggesting a cease fire between us. "You're a real firecracker. If you got to know me, you'd see I'm a nice guy, one of the good ones."

If I had a nickel for every time I heard those words ... I wouldn't say I'd be rich, but ...

Looking at him now in his tailored suit, striped tie, and leather shoes, I wasn't the only one in the perfect profession.

"There's no need to get upset, you know," he said. "We're just two people having a conversation."

Incorrect.

We were *one* person trying to have a conversation the other wasn't interested in having.

"I'm not upset," I said. "Trust me when I say you don't want to see me that way either."

He slapped a hand against his pantleg, bent his head back, and laughed.

I thought he was going to make a snarky quip back, but he didn't. He looked me in the eye, holding my gaze for a few seconds. It was almost like he'd seen something in my expression, something that made him see there was a lot more going on beneath the surface than he realized.

Which, of course, was correct.

"I apologize if I've offended you in any way, Georgiana," he said.

"What are you sorry for—coming here and teasing me about having a source who's feeding you information but not giving me his name?"

He frowned. "I guess. I had no idea you'd take it this way. I'd like to start over, hit the reset button on our conversation."

"Without a name, I can't start over."

"I can see now that it was wrong of me to come here, wrong

of me to mention my source in the first place. The idea that I know a little more about the case than I should compromises the person who gave me the information. If I give you his name, it could cause trouble for me and for him. I suppose I hadn't thought that through when I opened my mouth."

He sighed, rubbing a hand across his jaw, like he was disappointed in himself—but not for coming across information pertinent to the case, I presumed. Rather, he'd allowed his egotistical *I know what you've been up to* attitude get the better of him. And it was too late. The genie was out of the bottle.

"You say giving me a name will cause trouble if you do," I said. "I say it will cause trouble if you don't."

I reached into my pocket, pulling out my cell phone.

"Who are you calling?" he asked.

"Chief Foley. Maybe the three of us should have a chat about your source. You're withholding something from me. You've admitted as much."

"Oh, for goodness' sake. Put the phone down."

"Why should I?"

"As a gesture of my good faith, and to prove my intentions are only about wanting to see this case solved, I'll give you his name."

It wasn't a gesture of good faith.

It was him being backed into a corner, a corner he'd put himself in.

I set the phone next to me and leaned back, waiting.

He took a deep breath in and said, "He's a good kid. It's not his fault, okay? I asked him to poke around."

"His name?"

"Donovan Cole."

The name sounded familiar, but I couldn't place it.

And then it came to me.

"Isn't he a reporter for the county paper?" I asked.

"Yes, he is. In fact, I helped him get the job."

"I'm beginning to understand what's happening here. You helped him get his job, and he's helping you by feeding you information. Am I right?"

"It's nothing as scandalous as you're suggesting. He knows about my interest in this investigation. He's just as interested."

"He's been following me, hasn't he?"

Benjamin raised a brow. "I wouldn't know anything about that."

"What information has Donovan given you?"

"He knows you found evidence the police missed inside Cordelia Bennett's house."

"How did he come by this information?" I asked.

"I'm not sure. He didn't say, and I didn't ask. Is it true? Did you find a new piece of evidence?"

I thought about my conversation with Rosalyn the morning before and how I'd heard rustling in the bushes nearby. And then there was the feeling that came over me as I walked to Kayla's house, a feeling like I was being watched. It seemed I was being watched *and* followed. As to how the kid knew what he knew, that was easy for me to figure out. The windows in Kayla's house had been open during our conversation.

How much had the kid heard?

And was he prepared to write about it?

The mere thought of it made me nauseous.

"Where is Donovan now?" I asked.

"I don't know."

"Why don't you call him and find out? I'm guessing you have his phone number."

"Yes, I have it, but I'm not going to do that, Georgiana."

"Fine, I'll figure out where he is, and we'll have a little chat."

"I would appreciate it if you didn't."

"I don't appreciate being followed," I said, jabbing a finger at him for emphasis. "But I was, and I need to make sure it never happens again."

Benjamin leaned forward, resting his arms on his legs. "Cordelia was spying on her neighbors. Seems she saw some things she shouldn't have. You've spoken with the wives of both neighbors. Which one murdered her?"

"Who murdered Cordelia is still being investigated, and as for this conversation ... it's over."

25

The moment Donovan locked eyes on me when I exited the car, he turned and began sprinting in the opposite direction. He was young, in his twenties I guessed, and he had a face that reminded me of a ferret. While scrawny, he was quick on his feet. Given the heeled shoes I'd chosen to wear that morning weren't ideal, I kicked them off and chased after him.

In my mind, I told myself I was fast enough to catch him. In reality, he was a lot nimbler than I'd expected. Running after him, barefoot, on the sidewalk, didn't feel great. My lucky break came when he glanced back just long enough to assess the distance between us. Just for long enough a time that he tripped over a child's scooter and flew over it, tumbling to the ground.

I caught up to him, waited for him to catch his breath, and then I reached down, offering him a hand.

He looked up at me, shielding his face with his hand like he feared I might strike him.

"Take my hand, Donovan," I said, "And no more running, okay?"

Donovan accepted the hand I'd offered but didn't make eye

contact. When I got him back on his feet again, he bowed his head and said, "Sorry."

"If you're sorry, why did you run?"

"I was ... I don't know. I saw you, and it was the first thing that came to mind."

"I just want to talk."

"I can't believe Benjamin sold me out."

"I'm not sure why you're surprised. Benjamin's a politician in every sense of the word. If you haven't learned that by now, you better."

"Guess you're right."

"You've been following me."

"No, I haven't."

I crossed my arms, gritting my teeth as I said, "You know what would be great? You being honest with me. It would make my life a whole lot easier. Then we wouldn't have to go back and forth about what's the truth and what isn't. You followed me yesterday, and we both know it."

"Okay, so ... maybe I did. What are you going to do about it?"

His tone was more humble than arrogant.

"I haven't decided what to do about it yet," I said.

Donovan glanced down at his phone, which had flown out of his hand when he tripped and smashed onto the sidewalk. The glass had shattered into a million pieces. He reached down, cursing as he picked it up. He pressed a few buttons, trying to get the screen to come alive, but there was only the black screen of death.

He cursed a few more times, this time toward the sky, but even the heavens couldn't help him.

"My recordings, I can't believe they're ..."

He slapped a hand against his mouth, as if realizing he'd said something he shouldn't have.

"You *recorded* me?" I asked.

"I never said I recorded *you*. They could be recordings of anything."

We were back to where we started. Donovan denying what he'd done, and me struggling to get to the truth.

"You recorded me, and if I had to guess *what* you recorded, it would be the conversation I had with Cordelia's neighbor, Kayla," I said.

"I ... I just wanted to be sure I had my facts straight about what was going on in the investigation so far."

His hands were trembling.

"So, you've been stalking me, and—"

"I wasn't *stalking* you," he said. "This may sound crazy, but I am in awe of you, the way you do things, and how you get people to tell you stuff. If anything, I want to learn from you, learn your process."

Flattery didn't faze me most of the time but the sincerity in his voice was something I couldn't ignore. Not to mention the way he kept offering me quick, fleeting glances and then looking away. He reminded me of a timid boy who'd just met his celebrity crush.

"Listen, you can't record conversations in California," I said. "You're a reporter, and you know that. It's a two-party consent state. You need *my* consent to record the conversation *and* Kayla's consent, and I'm never going to give it to you. If the recording is gone because your phone is broken, consider it a good thing."

"I wasn't going to record you, at first. I mean it."

"Then why did you?"

"Has anyone ever told you you're a fast talker? I was taking notes, and I couldn't keep up. Recording you so I could replay it later seemed like a good solution at the time."

If I was a speed talker, it was news to me.

"I'm sorry if I upset you," he said. "I never meant for any of this to happen, and I wasn't going to report on anything you said."

"If you weren't going to report it, you wouldn't have recorded me."

"When I started the recording, I had no idea what was about to be said. I thought it was just going to be a basic interview, until it wasn't. I didn't expect to hear most of what I heard."

"Who else have you spoken to about my conversation with Kayla?"

"Just Benjamin."

"I'm not sure I believe you."

"It's true. I'll do anything to make it up to you. Just tell me what you want, what I can do to make things right."

I thought about what I wanted and came up with a few things.

"The first thing you're going to do is to stop following me," I said. "I want you to keep quiet about what you know. There are to be no more conversations about this case with Benjamin, understand?"

"I do. Are you gonna ... you know, turn me in for what I did?"

"After Benjamin came to my office, my first thought was to stop by the chief of police's office and tell him what Benjamin knew. Then I decided I'd come straight to your house first and hear what you had to say. There aren't always two sides to a story, but in this case, I believe there was a bit of coercion on Benjamin's part."

The longer our conversation went on, the more I found myself liking the kid. He was awkward and a little shy, and against my better judgment, I believed his apology was sincere.

We turned, heading back toward his house.

"I'll make you a deal," I said. "If you promise to honor what we discussed today, I won't say anything to anyone else about what you did. But I better not see anything in the paper or catch you following me again."

"I won't."

"Good. Don't give me a reason to change my mind."

He breathed a sigh of relief. "Can I ask you a question, off the record?"

"Donovan, anything we're talking about right now is off the record."

"Of course, you're right. I'm sorry."

"You don't have to keep apologizing."

"All right, sorry." He shook his head. "Dang it, I did it again."

Unable to hold back, I laughed. "You seem nervous."

"I guess I am," he said. "I've been following your career, but I meant what I said ... I'm not stalking you. I'm more of an admirer."

"Why?"

"I want to be like you, I guess. Lame, I know."

"It isn't."

"For as long as I can remember, I've wanted to be a detective. I don't think I have what it takes."

"How do you know until you try?"

"I'm no good with people, not in the way you are."

"I don't believe it," I said. "In the field you're in, you can't be a good reporter if you're not."

"I've been working on it ... on my people skills."

I leaned to the side, nudging his shoulder. "You want my advice?"

"Please."

"The first thing you could do to improve your people skills is not to run when a person confronts you."

"I wouldn't have if ... Okay, the reason I did is because Benjamin called me before you got here. When he told me what you said to him and how you said it, I was worried. I figured you were so mad, you might throat-punch me or something."

Giving him a nice, hard slap to the face when I caught up to him had crossed my mind. But I did my best to behave like a lady, which came with its challenges.

"I don't know what you've heard about me, but I don't go around throat-punching people." I reached my car and opened the door. "Keep at it, the journalist thing. I'm sure it will get better. And if it doesn't, you're young. You have plenty of time to change your career path."

"I'll try. Before you go, I ... ahh, I was hoping to ask you a question."

"Go on."

"What do you think about, like ... letting me tag along with you? I won't say a word, and I won't write anything for the paper unless you say it's okay."

Given what we'd just discussed, it was a bold question.

"I'd say you've pressed your luck enough for one day," I said. "For now, let's leave things where they are."

I checked in with Phoebe to see how she'd been doing since I saw her last. She sounded better, and she'd even made an appointment to speak to a therapist about what she was going through. I offered to take her to lunch, but she'd already made plans with Foley, so we set up a lunch date for a few days from now.

After speaking to Donovan earlier, I noticed I had a missed call from Claudette. I wasn't looking forward to calling her back, even though she deserved an update on the progress I was making, or lack thereof. I wasn't far enough along in the investigation to give her the answers she wanted. And even though it had only been two days since she hired me, in her eyes, I was sure she would view it as plenty of time to uncover some solid information.

I entered the address of my next stop into my phone, and then I gave Claudette a call. We chatted for several minutes, and I admitted I'd found a note that led me to believe Cordelia had been spying on at least one of her neighbors. She asked if I thought one of them could be her sister's killer. I said I didn't know, which was the truth. I didn't. Not yet.

I gave Claudette a brief overview of Cordelia's notes, thinking she'd chime in and give me her own opinion about them, but she didn't. She said it was best not to point a finger in any direction until we were certain the finger was pointed in the right one.

I agreed.

We ended the call, and I pulled into a parking space in front of Eco Earth. The building itself was impressive, a three-story, polished white brick with oversized windows.

I entered through the front door and looked around. Several feet in front of me was the receptionist's desk. A young woman sat behind it, typing on her computer keyboard at warp speed. She was dressed in a simple black dress, and she wore a pair of big, red, round eyeglasses. Her hair was pulled back into a tight bun and secured with a fastener that reminded me of chopsticks.

I approached her, and she didn't acknowledge me at first, her focus on the computer screen in front of her. Once she stopped typing, she looked up, and I noted the nameplate pinned to her dress.

"Hi, Nadia," I said.

"Hi. Can I help you with something?"

"I would like to speak to the person in charge."

She considered my request and then leaned toward me, removing her glasses. She looked me up and down like she was trying to figure out what I was doing there and why I wanted to speak to her supervisor.

"Is Tripp expecting you?" she asked.

"He is not."

"I'm not sure he can see you, then. He's a busy man. We have a lot going on here today."

"I understand," I said. "Maybe it would help if I explained why I'm here."

She nodded. "Maybe it would."

"My name is Georgiana Germaine. I'm a private detective, and I'm investigating a murder that took place in Cambria a couple of weeks ago."

Her eyes widened, and she perked up, her voice raising a few octaves. "Are you talking about the old lady who died in the library?"

"I am."

"I see. Why are you here?"

"One of the murder victim's neighbors works for Eco Earth."

"Which one?"

"Eddy Westwood."

As soon as I uttered his name, she sprang from her chair, pointing a finger in my direction. "You stay here. I'll ... umm, I'll be right back."

Nadia rounded the corner, disappearing into a long corridor. I did what she asked, staying in place, drumming my fingers along the top of the desk as I waited.

A few minutes later, she returned with a tall, lanky man at her side. He was dressed in a dingy, white, button-up shirt, blue slacks, and white tennis shoes.

Nadia tipped her head in my direction, turned toward the man, and said, "That's her."

He walked toward me, extending a hand. "Miss Germaine, I'm Tripp Redding. Would you mind following me please?"

His tone was serious enough that I wondered if following him might be a bad idea. I did so anyway, walking side by side with him back through the corridor until he stopped at the elevator.

He stepped inside and turned, asking me if I would please, "Get in."

Once I did, he pushed the third-floor button, and then folded his hands together in front of him, remaining silent.

The elevator doors opened, and Tripp extended a hand, saying, "Right this way, Miss Germaine."

"I'd like to know where we're going."

"To my office. We'll talk further once we're there."

Tripp with his monotone voice seemed like a no-nonsense kind of guy, which was appealing to me in ways. I much preferred dealing with someone who was direct than a person who gave me the runaround.

He passed a few offices and then stopped in front of a door, swiping the keycard around his neck in front of a square, gray panel. The box's frame lit up a bright-green color, and the office door opened.

I stepped inside and looked around. The office took up a majority of the third floor, and most of it was unused space—carpeting with no furniture or accessories of any kind. In the far left corner, a desk faced the window. Through it, he had a perfect view of the parking lot, and anyone who was coming or going.

"Go ahead and have a seat, if you don't mind," he said.

"I don't mind at all."

"Nadia tells me you're investigating the Bennett murder, and you're a private detective?"

"I am."

"I understand the woman who died lived next to one of our former employees."

I was taken aback.

"What do you mean *former* employees?" I asked. "I was under the impression Eddy still works here."

"Why would you be under such an impression?"

"I spoke with Eddy's wife yesterday. He wasn't home at the time. When I asked her where he was and when she expected him, she said he was at work, and she didn't know when he would return home."

Tripp leaned forward, folding his arms over his desk. "How interesting."

"I feel like I'm missing some information here," I said. "Can you fill me in?"

"Not much to fill in."

If I wanted answers, it was clear I was going to have to do the legwork myself. "When was the last time you saw Eddy?"

"I haven't seen him in ... oh, let's see now ... has to be a couple of weeks, maybe longer."

"Any idea why Rosalyn would tell me Eddy worked here if he doesn't?"

"None at all. It's rather strange, don't you think?"

I did.

"When was the last time you spoke with Eddy?" I asked.

He was just about to respond, but he hesitated for a few beats. Then, "Ah, yes," like a lightbulb moment had occurred.

Tripp opened his desk drawer, taking out a large leather planner. He opened it, flipping through and running a finger up and down the pages as he read.

Several flips later, he said, "To answer your question, the last time we spoke was sixteen days ago. I remember the conversation well, including the date, because it was the last day I worked before I left for a family vacation."

"What did you and Eddy talk about?"

"Can't go into too much detail, as some of it was confidential, work-related information."

"What can you tell me?"

Tripp drummed his fingers on the desk a couple of times before starting. "Eddy came to my office to speak to me, and he was upset, flailing his arms, yelling. It was hard to get through to him. I've never known him to be so unreasonable before. It was a side of him I'd never seen."

"Can I ask why he was so upset?"

"There's an employee he worked with here, someone he demanded I fire. I don't feel comfortable giving you the employee's name, but Eddy said he wouldn't work one more day with the guy."

"Why not?"

"He was ranting, going in circles, giving me tidbits of information, but even then, it took a while before it all started to make sense. What I got out of the conversation was that this particular employee had offended him in some way by speaking to his wife."

"What did the guy say to her?" I asked.

"I'm not sure what was said, but I can imagine. Eddy's wife had dropped him off at work that morning, and this employee had a brief conversation with her. Then she left. From what I gather, some flirting had gone on—not on Eddy's wife's end, but on the employee's end."

"How do you know?"

"After Eddy came to my office, I spoke with the employee. He admitted he thought Mrs. Westwood was a real looker, and he'd told her as much. In his mind, his comments were fine. He wasn't aware that Nadia, our receptionist, had overheard the entire conversation. She confronted him and told him she thought the way he'd behaved with Eddy's wife was inappropriate. He laughed it off, saying something about her being too stuffy, which fueled the fire. She went to Eddy and told him what had happened."

"What did you say after Eddy demanded you fire the guy?" I asked.

"I said I'd have to think about it. I thought he'd simmer down, and we could revisit the issue once I returned from my vacation. I planned to bring both men in and see if we could resolve the situation. On my first day back to the office, I was told Eddy hadn't shown up to work since that day.

"Did you or anyone else call him to find out why he hadn't returned to work?"

"I assumed he quit and hadn't bothered to tell anyone. I felt bad about downplaying the situation. So, to answer your question ... yes, I called him. Several times, in fact."

"Did you speak to him?"

Tripp shook his head. "Eddy never answered the phone. It rang and rang and went to voicemail. I left messages, but he never got back to me."

"You didn't happen to call his wife, did you?"

"No, I didn't, but funny thing is, your timing's perfect. I planned on calling her today."

"Why now?"

"A couple of days ago, we hired someone to fill Eddy's position. I asked Nadia to check Eddy's locker to make sure it was cleaned out. I planned on letting Eddy's replacement use it. When she opened the locker, she was surprised to find Eddy had left some things behind."

"Like what?"

"A couple of thermoses, a pair of shoes, two shirts, and a watch—a Rolex. All this time I figured he didn't want to show his face around here again, not even to gather his things. But I can't imagine leaving a Rolex behind. Can you?"

I *couldn't* imagine leaving a Rolex watch behind, so before I'd left Eco Earth, I asked if I could see the watch. Tripp agreed to show it to me, and I snapped a few photos, sending them to Hunter so she could do some research on it. When she got back to me, I learned the watch was a current year model, with a price tag of twelve thousand dollars. I could think of only one reason such a watch would have been left behind—he had no choice but to leave it.

Had Eddy murdered Cordelia, and now he was in hiding?

After my discussion with Tripp, I knew where I needed to go next, and I drove straight to Rosalyn's house. I stood at the door for a few minutes, knocking, but no one answered, and the dog didn't bark either. I walked over to the garage, standing on my tiptoes to peer through one of the small panes of glass running along the top of it. There were no vehicles parked in the garage.

I went back to the front door and tried the doorknob. The door was locked, and the last time I'd been there, I'd noticed it had a sturdy deadbolt, one that wouldn't allow me to pry the door open without significant effort. I walked around the outside of the house, pulling on windows to see if I could get any of the latches to budge. None of them did.

As I made my way to the backyard, I spotted a shed—if one could call it that. It was old and dilapidated, and some of the wood planks had started to detach from the structure. The shed looked like it had been built around the time the house had been. And unlike the modern doors and windows of the main house, the shed had a simple latch, and no lock.

I flipped the latch open and stepped inside. It was mid-afternoon but given the shed didn't appear to have any electricity, it was hard to see, even with the door all the way open. But I could see enough—with the help of my phone's flashlight.

There were several gallons of paint resting on the dusty wooden shelves, gardening tools, a rusty toolbox, and a lawnmower. I walked over to the shelves to get a closer look, using my cell phone's flashlight to look around.

On one of the dust-filled shelves, there was a clean spot in the shape of a square, like something that had rested there in recent days was now gone.

I spent a few more minutes looking around, and, finding nothing else of note, I exited the shed. I had almost made it to my car when a black Mercedes pulled alongside, its horn beeping. The passenger-side window came down, and my mother shouted, "Yoo-hoo!"

Octavia was behind the wheel. She offered me a wave, and as I neared the car, I noticed they were all dressed up.

"Where are you two headed?" I asked.

"A campaign fundraiser dinner in San Luis Obispo," my mother said.

"You look nice."

"Thank you, dear. What are you doing at Rosalyn's house?"

"I had a few questions for her, but it doesn't look like she's home."

"Can't say I've seen her around much, but I've been a busy bee. How's the investigation going?"

I thought about waiting, speaking to her later, but so much was running through my mind, I couldn't help myself.

"Yesterday, when I was talking to Rosalyn, she told me her husband works at a company called Eco Earth," I said. "I was just there, and I spoke to his boss. Eddy hasn't shown up for work in weeks."

My mother crossed her arms. "Well, you did say you thought she'd been lying to you."

"I was hoping to get the truth out of her, but since she's not here, it will have to wait."

"Any other leads you're following up on?"

I thought about whether I wanted to talk about the notes Cordelia had left inside of the Agatha Christie novel, and I decided against it.

"Did Cordelia ever talk about any of her neighbors when you were together?" I asked.

My mother gave the question some thought. "Not too much. She seemed to get on all right with them ... well, except for Eddy. She wasn't fond of him. I'm sure her dislike of him was for the same reasons I don't like him either. He's a rude man."

"What about Seth? Did she ever mention him?"

"She found him a bit peculiar."

"In what way?"

"One day he'd strike up a conversation, and the next, he ignored her. It's like he has two personalities, a bit of a Jekyll and Hyde. Well, I suppose he's more Jekyll than Hyde, or Kayla wouldn't stay married to him, would she now?"

"I guess you haven't heard," I said.

"What haven't I heard?"

"They're getting a divorce."

My mother pressed a hand to her chest. "Oh, dear. I wonder

if that's what she wanted to talk to me about. She stopped by the house yesterday, but I wasn't home. I've had so much going on, I haven't made time for much else. I'll pop over later on and speak with her."

"When I spoke to Seth, he told me he was friends with Cordelia."

"*Friends*? That's a stretch."

"He said he checked in on her from time to time after Marlon died, and Cordelia gave him books to read."

"I wouldn't know anything about it." She paused, then added, "Come to think of it, I saw him leaving her house ... oh, I guess it would have been three or four weeks ago now."

"Did he see you?"

"Sure did. I waved. He waved back. Wasn't much more to it. He did have a book in hand, so I suppose she could have been loaning books to him, as you say. Still, it seems to me he was more of an acquaintance than a friend."

Octavia leaned over, smiling up at me as she said, "You're welcome to attend the fundraiser tonight as my guest. It's at the Balenciaga House."

"Oh, yes," my mother said. "The food they're serving will be top notch."

It was a tempting offer, but I'd had a long day, and there was still one more stop I wanted to make before heading home.

"I appreciate the invite, but I still have a bit more work to do," I said.

"You get so caught up in your cases, you don't take enough time for yourself," my mother said.

"I have one more item on the agenda for today, and then I plan on stopping for the rest of the night."

"Good, a little rest goes a long way. I'm glad I ran into you. I've been meaning to thank you for looking in on your sister."

"When did you talk to Phoebe?" I asked.

"Last night. As soon as she gave me the news about the miscarriage, I wanted to drive straight over. She said she wasn't up for visitors, though, and she just wanted to relax. It took everything in me to honor her wishes, but I did."

My mother grabbed a tissue from her handbag, blotting her eyes.

"She's going to be all right, Mom."

She reached out a hand and grabbed mine. "I know she will, because she has us, and she's strong, just like you were when it happened to you."

The conversation was taking an uncomfortable turn. Going down Unwanted Memory Lane had no appeal to me.

My mother seemed to pick up on it, and she said, "We best get going. Tell Giovanni I said hello and give Luka a big hug from me."

"Will do."

"Best of luck on your investigation," Octavia said. "I hope it will all be over soon."

She put the car in gear, and as they headed down the street, my mother leaned her head out the window, blowing me a kiss as she shouted, "Tootles!"

28

"It's like I told your work partner, Simone—my wife doesn't want to see anyone," Mack said.

Samantha's husband was a tall fellow. His skin had a leathery, sun kissed look to it, and he had a thick accent I couldn't place, perhaps German.

"I understand Samantha hasn't wanted to leave home ever since the night Cordelia died," I said. "I stopped by to see if she's all right."

"She isn't. She feels responsible for what happened to Cordelia."

"Why? It's not her fault."

"I know, I've told her as much. I'm sure you know Samantha was supposed to close the library that night. Because she allowed Cordelia to do it, she feels a sense of responsibility for her death."

"I don't think it would have made a difference," I said. "I believe it was a targeted hit."

Mack shook his head, exhaling a sigh. "Why target a librarian?"

"I hope to have answers about why she was murdered soon.

Listen, I know your wife hasn't wanted to leave the house since Cordelia died, but we've talked before, and I was hoping—"

"I'm aware of the conversation between you, Detective Whitlock, and my wife on that dreadful night."

"When she showed up as we were gathering evidence, she was in shock over what had happened. We chatted with her inside Whitlock's vehicle hoping to calm her emotions, in that moment, at least. I thought if I stopped by tonight, I could let her know about the leads I have in the case. Maybe it will help her feel better."

He stared at me for a time, as if trying to decide what to do with me. "I appreciate your consideration of her. Still, I don't think she'll see you."

"It's worth a try."

"Might I ask how strong your leads are? Do you have a prime suspect?"

More than one.

"Cordelia's sister hired me to investigate a couple of days ago, and yes, I do feel I'm heading in the right direction," I said.

"I don't suppose you'd like to share any information you've discovered with me?"

"Not until I'm confident I have the right person."

He raised a brow. "So you have a suspect, but you have doubts whether said person committed the murder."

Yes, that's why they're called suspects.

"I'm working on proving my theories," I said. "It shouldn't be long before I do."

Part of me wanted to give him a small detail, nothing too deep, just enough to provide me with an opportunity to get past him and speak to Samantha. As I contemplated the best path forward, I saw a shadow flicker behind him. I tipped my head to the side, peering down the hallway at a despondent, disheveled Samantha. She looked surprised to see me as she walked toward us, her eyes red and puffy. She was dressed in a plain, white, V-neck tee and baggy, gray sweatpants, and her hair was tangled and messy, like it hadn't been brushed today.

"Hey, Samantha," I said. "I stopped by to see how you were doing."

She nodded but said nothing.

Mack wrapped an arm around her shoulders, pulling her close. "It's okay, honey."

"No, Mack. It isn't."

I felt guilty for being there, like I'd done something wrong. She was worse off than I'd imagined. And while I believed her guilt for not closing up the library herself had something to do with it, it seemed to me like she was taking it too hard—like there was a secondary explanation for her behavior.

Stemming from those thoughts, I considered a way to evoke a deeper conversation from her, but then I decided for tonight, I'd keep it simple for now. What would happen if I retreated instead of pushed?

"I'm sorry to have bothered you both this evening," I said. "I think I should go. Samantha, we can talk another time when you're feeling more up to having visitors, okay?"

I reached into my pocket, grabbing my car keys.

Mack's expression softened, and I could see relief in his eyes.

I started for my car, and Samantha stepped outside, saying, "Georgiana, wait."

It seemed my casual attitude may have paid off, and I faced her.

"There's a reason why I'm struggling so much right now," she said.

"I wish you weren't. There's nothing for you to feel guilty about. What happened to Cordelia isn't your fault."

"You're wrong. It *is* my fault. You don't understand."

"I'd like to understand, if you're up to talking to me."

Mack placed a hand on her shoulder. "You don't have to do this right now, all right?"

"Yes, I do," she said. "I should have done it in the beginning, the night Cordelia was murdered. I was a coward then. I won't be a coward now."

"Whatever it is, you can tell me," I said.

"If I do, you'll never see me the same way again, and I wouldn't blame you."

"I'm a lot more understanding than most people think," I said. "And I'm a good listener."

A tear trailed down her cheek, and she flicked it away.

"It's obvious you've been keeping something in," I said. "I've done it myself, on more than one occasion. I can tell you from personal experience, it won't get any better until you get it out."

"You're right. I've been keeping something from everyone because of the shame I feel about it. I saw someone in the library on the day Cordelia died, someone who didn't fit in."

"In what way didn't the person fit in?"

She looked me in the eye, frowning as she said, "In every possible way."

29

Samantha invited me inside, and I walked with her and Mack to the kitchen. I sat down on a barstool, and she turned toward her husband, saying, "I believe I'm going to need a cocktail for this conversation."

"Anything you want, honey," he said. "What's it going to be?"

"I'll have my usual."

He nodded and turned his attention to me. "What about you? We have wine, beer, gin, tea, coffee, soda ... and water, of course."

Given I was planning on heading home after our visit, to wind down and enjoy a couple of drinks with Giovanni, I kept it simple and asked for a glass of water.

Mack stopped as he passed by Samantha, bending toward her and planting a kiss on her forehead. She gave his hand a squeeze, and then he proceeded to open one of the kitchen cabinets, whistling as he said, "One strawberry margarita, coming right up."

While the cocktail was being made, Samantha sat down next to me. I was hoping she would continue the conversation we'd been having before, but she went quiet. It was possible she was trying to work up the nerve to continue what she'd started. And although I didn't want to push, I was tired, and I had little gas left in my peopling tank.

We chitchatted about topics of no consequence, and then Mack brought over her cocktail. She put the straw in her mouth and sipped and sipped and sipped, finishing half of it. Then she set the glass on the counter. "Mack, would you mind leaving the two of us alone for a few minutes, honey?"

Based on his furrowed brow, he did mind—and not just a little—a lot.

"I'd like to stay," he said. "I believe it would be for the best. Don't you agree?"

"I understand why, but I'll be fine," she said. "I promise."

He stood there for a long second, not saying anything. Then he did as she asked, exiting the kitchen and making sure she knew he would be in the den if she needed anything.

When Mack was out of earshot, Samantha said, "I've told Mack what I'm about to tell you, but I didn't give him much in the way of details."

I considered telling her to take her time, but in truth, all I wanted was for it to come out. The faster, the better.

"What is it you need to tell me?" I asked.

She downed the rest of the margarita, slid off the barstool, and took the glass to the kitchen sink. Turning on the faucet, she rinsed it off, and put it in the dishwasher. Then she opened a cupboard and grabbed a shot glass and a bottle of tequila. She poured a single shot and offered me one.

I declined.

"Suit yourself," she said.

She swigged back the entire shot and then breathed a long sigh as she returned to the barstool.

"I believe I'm ready now," she said.

Good.

I'd been ready for what felt like ages.

"It started out as a quiet, slow day in the library," she began. "There's often a lag time in the middle of it, and sometimes no one else is there except us—the employees who work there, which is me, Cordelia, and Johnny. I'd just started putting some books on the shelves, and I heard the front door open and close. I looked over to see who'd come in, and I saw a man. He was tall and muscular, and he didn't look like the usual type of person who comes in. Everything about him stood out."

"Can you explain why?"

"He was wearing dark sunglasses, and he had his long hair in a ponytail, which he'd pulled through the opening in the back of his ballcap. He also wore a black leather vest over a black T-shirt like he was in a motorcycle gang, except the pants he was wearing looked like nice dress slacks. His entire look seemed so odd to me, but I suppose I don't know what's trendy these days."

"Do you remember what time he entered the library?"

"I'd say it was early afternoon, between one and two."

"Did the man acknowledge you, or did you acknowledge him?" I asked.

"When he first came in, he was glancing around, and he saw me staring at him. He tipped his head toward me, but he didn't say anything. Then he disappeared into one of the aisles. Because I was preoccupied with what I was doing, and he was so quiet, I forgot about him for a while."

"And then?"

"I was walking to the front desk, and I saw him sitting in one of the chairs on the opposite end of the room, by the window. He had a book in his hand, and he was reading. Well, to clarify, I assumed he was reading at first. When I think back on it now, it seems to me he wasn't focused on the book at all."

"What *was* he focused on?"

"He was looking around, watching people come in and out, that kind of thing."

"Where was Cordelia at the time?"

"She was standing in the romance section, talking to Johnny."

"Did the guy ever pay any specific attention to Cordelia while he was there?"

Samantha shrugged. "He may have. I'm not sure."

"Did any of you talk to him?"

She pointed a finger at herself. "I did."

"When?"

"If I had to guess, I'd say it was about an hour after he arrived. I wasn't sure why he was hanging around and not leaving. And given he didn't seem interested in the book in his hand, I went over to have a chat with him."

"What did you say?"

She tapped a finger to the counter, thinking. "I mentioned I hadn't ever seen him come in before. He said he'd just moved to the area, and I suggested he apply for a library card. He told me he already had one, but I doubt that. As we were talking, I glanced down at the book in his hand. In all the time he'd been sitting there, he'd only turned a few of its pages."

"What was the book?"

"I couldn't tell, and before we could chat any further, the phone rang, and I went to the desk to answer it. When I returned, the book was gone, and so was he."

I had to admit, it did seem suspicious.

But the fact she found the man odd didn't make him a murderer.

"I understand why the timing of a strange man you've never seen before coming into the library seems suspect," I said. "Maybe it is, and maybe it isn't. Either way, you can't blame yourself for any part of what happened."

"I *did* do something wrong, though. I should have given you this information the night she died, and I didn't."

"Why did you wait until now?"

"When I learned about what happened to her, I was in shock, to be honest. I hadn't processed all that had gone on that day yet. When I did, I realized I needed to say something, to tell someone, even if it amounted to nothing. I let my fear stop me from doing the right thing."

"What are you afraid of, Samantha?"

She choked up, struggling to get out the words. "I've had nightmares ever since she died, nightmares of me telling the police, and word getting around town about that strange man. What if he was the one who killed her? If he finds out I've been running my mouth, what's to stop him from coming after me?"

While I understood Samantha's concern for her own safety, I didn't find much merit in it—that the killer would return to shut her mouth for good. Still, she'd let me know there was one other person in the library that day who may have seen him—Johnny, the other employee.

I wanted nothing more than to return home after the long day I'd had, but I knew if I didn't make one more one last stop, I'd regret it.

When I pulled up to Johnny's driveway, a burgundy '90s Mercury Capri two-door hatchback was parked in the driveway. After too many years in the sun, the paint on its roof was weathered and faded, adding to the rundown look of the vehicle.

As I glanced at Johnny's condo, I noticed the blinds were drawn. Even so, light was emanating from between the slats, a good sign that he was at home. I parked behind the Capri and walked to the front door, ringing the doorbell.

I heard some rustling from inside the house but got distracted when I felt something brush across my ankles. I looked down. A cat was rubbing itself over my legs, purring up at me as if in need of attention. It was a big, white, overweight fluffball, but its bright-blue eyes were captivating, and before I knew it I was crouching down, stroking its fur.

The front door opened, and the man looked down, smiling at the cat and then at me. I gave the cat one last pat and stood, facing the man in front of me.

"Hello," I said.

"Hiya. What can I do for you?"

"I'm Georgiana Germaine with the Case Closed Detective Agency. Are you Johnny?"

"That's me. Why?"

"I've been hired to investigate Cordelia's—"

"I know who you are. You work with that woman ... Simone Bonet."

"I do. I believe the two of you spoke yesterday."

"We didn't talk long, a few minutes at most."

He turned his head, peering inside his house as if something had diverted his attention.

"Is everything okay?" I asked.

"Aww, yeah. It's fine."

He had a thick Southern accent, which I enjoyed, but it was hard to make out what he was saying at times.

"I was wondering if I could speak to you for a few minutes," I said.

"Why?"

"I just visited with Samantha, and I wanted to ask you about the last day you worked with Cordelia at the library."

His eyes lit up. "*You* saw Samantha? I was told she wouldn't see anyone, not since the murder. How's she doing?"

"Better, I hope. There was something she hadn't told me before now. It's the reason why I came to see you. I have a few questions."

He looked at me, then at the ground, then back to me again,

as if trying to decide what to say. "I see. I suppose you better come in, then."

He opened the door all the way, turned, and I followed him to what I could only describe as a living room turned into a game room. There were a couple of pinball machines, a shuffleboard, and a pool table. The ideal bachelor pad.

In the center of said bachelor pad was a sofa and two chairs, each covered in tight plastic wrap, custom made to fit the furniture perfectly. Johnny suggested I take a seat, but as I assessed the meager offerings, all I could focus on was how much cat hair was around—on the furniture, the floor, in the air.

He sat on one of the chairs and squinted up at me, saying, "I think I know what this visit is all about."

"Why do you think I'm here?" I asked.

"You tell me."

I'd played a few games in my life when trying to extract information, but *you tell me* was a game I had no interest playing.

"You had a conversation at work with Cordelia on the day she died," I said. "In the afternoon, in the romance section."

"I suppose I was one of the last people who talked to her before she, umm ... she, umm ... anyway, I don't know what Samantha told you, but yes, it's true. We argued."

Samantha had made no mention of an argument.

If it had been a heated argument, I assumed she would have seen it or overheard it or both.

Had she known about the argument between them and what it was about?

And if so ... why had she kept it from me?

Was she covering for Johnny?

"Why did the two of you argue?" I asked.

"I, for one, don't shy away from the principles I believe in."

It was more of a statement than an answer.

"Having principles is one thing," I said. "Having an argument is another."

"Do you have any leads in your investigation, Detective?"

He was attempting to divert the conversation.

It wouldn't work.

"A few leads, yes," I said.

"Then why are you here, putting a target on *my* back?"

"I'm not targeting you. I'm just here to chat, nothing more."

To keep him talking, the right chess moves needed to be played. I leaned into his preconceived notion that I'd arrived at his house with full knowledge of the argument he'd had with Cordelia.

"I heard Cordelia could be argumentative at times," I said.

A lie, of course.

In truth, Cordelia seemed more avoidant than argumentative.

A Siamese cat crossed in front of him, and he bent down, pulling it into his arms. The cat offered up brief resistance, but Johnny either didn't seem to notice or didn't care. "The argument was the only one we ever had."

"I'd like to hear your side of the story."

"It wasn't a big deal. Not a big deal at all, no. No reason to make anything of it. No reason to talk about it either, in my opinion. I don't even know why Samantha brought it up to you. Why would she? What would be gained? People argue all the time. It's healthy for any relationship. Healthy is good. You know what I mean?"

As I stood there trying to piece together the speed round I'd just heard, I was reminded of the conversation I'd had with Simone. She'd described Johnny as a man who spoke fast, rambled, and went from one subject to the next. I was seeing that side of him now. While standing there, I'd taken the time to glance around when he wasn't making eye contact. On the kitchen counter, I'd spotted a few small baggies filled with white powder.

Maybe Simone was right.

Maybe Johnny did do drugs.

Based on his behavior, I guessed the baggies may have been filled with cocaine.

And he still hadn't told me what the argument was about.

"Why did you and Cordelia argue that day?" I asked.

"Oh, it wasn't a big deal."

"If it wasn't a big deal, I don't see why we can't talk about it."

"It's just … she liked to do things one way, and I like to do things another way. I was her superior, in every sense of the word. I've been working there for years. She'd just started. I didn't take kindly to her coming in and suggesting we do things in a different way just because she thought it would be better."

"What was she suggesting you change?"

"She had a bunch of ideas about how we could engage the community in new ways, things she'd heard other libraries were doing. She knew we lived in a small town. She knew we had a limited budget. I didn't understand why she was pushing something we couldn't accommodate. We didn't even know if the community would take to any of the ideas if we did try them."

"Was Samantha involved in the conversation?"

He nodded. "I guess I raised my voice a little more than she would have liked at one point. She came over and asked me to keep my voice down. I agreed. I wanted to end the conversation. Cordelia wasn't ready to, though. I started to walk away, and she came after me."

"What happened?"

"She wouldn't drop it, and I suppose it made me even more mad. There I was, willing to take the high road, and when she kept pushing her agenda, I lost it."

"Do you mean in a verbal way?"

"Of course. What do you take me for, lady? I'm no abuser. I've never laid a hand on a woman, just so we're clear."

"I wasn't suggesting you did."

Johnny put the cat down and went quiet, no doubt wanting to end the conversation. He was fidgeting with his fingers, like his nerves were getting the better of him. Maybe he needed a fix. Or maybe my line of questioning had pushed him further than he wanted to go.

I still wasn't getting the full picture of the argument they'd had or what ideas Cordelia suggested. I allowed the silence to go on for a time, watching him twitch and squirm in his chair. He didn't seem to enjoy the silence any more than I did.

"You know I'm not responsible for what happened to Cordelia, right?" he said. "I've already spoken to the police, and they cleared me, and of course they did, because I didn't do anything wrong."

They hadn't cleared anyone, to my knowledge, but I expected they'd offered him some assurance, making him believe he wasn't a suspect.

He was rubbing his hands together now, and I worried he was about ready to clam up. I switched subjects.

"When I was speaking to Samantha earlier, she told me there was a man in the library during the time of your conversation with Cordelia, someone she considered odd."

"People come in and out all day. What did he look like?"

"Tall, muscular, wearing a black leather vest, dress slacks. He was sitting off to the side, acting like he was reading a book when he wasn't, watching people come in and out. Do you recall seeing a man who fits that description?"

"Nope. Not a one."

"Are you sure?"

"Positive, though I'll admit, if a man came in during my chat with Cordelia, I could have been a little too irritated to notice.

When I get like that, I don't always see what's going on around me. Sorry."

I'd left Samantha's place feeling like the man she described was a great new lead, and in seconds, Johnny had me questioning things—questioning Samantha, and whether the man she'd mentioned even existed.

She'd kept me in the dark about the argument between Johnny and Cordelia.

What else was I being kept in the dark about?

31

I was curled up on the couch next to Giovanni and Luka watching *Shark Tank*, a show we frequently watched at night together. My body was spent, but my mind was active, and it showed no signs of slowing just yet.

After discussing the frustrations of my day, Giovanni agreed that nothing I'd learned so far seemed to fit together in the right way. And I was running out of people to question. As I sat with him now, snuggled beneath the arm he'd wrapped around my shoulders, I felt myself begin to fade at last, and Giovanni suggested we retire to the bedroom.

As we stood, my cell phone buzzed.

I glanced at the time.

It was past midnight.

No one would call at this hour, unless ...

"Is everything all right?" I said as I answered. "Is it Phoebe?"

"Your sister is just fine," Foley said. "She's sleeping."

"If you're not calling about her, what are you calling about?"

"I'm sorry, I know it's late."

"I assume there's something you need to tell me. What is it?"

"Your mother's neighbor, Eddy Westwood ... I know why he hasn't been home. The man's dead."

Dead.

That threw me for a loop, but it did explain why Eddy hadn't been to work and why he hadn't been seen at home in a while.

"How? When? What happened?" I asked.

"There was a power outage across town a couple of days back," Foley said.

"Yeah, I remember. It lasted a few hours."

"A resident who lives on Gardenia Street was walking her dog past her neighbor's house today, and she got a whiff of something horrible coming from the garage. She called us to check it out, but we've been so busy, we didn't get around to it until a couple of hours ago."

"Who owns the house?"

"Eddy and Rosalyn Westwood. They bought the house as an investment rental, had it up on VRBO and a few other places. Here's the kicker. Until a couple weeks ago, the house had been rented out on a consistent basis. It was almost always booked. In the past three weeks, the listing is showing as unavailable on the web page."

"What about future bookings?" I asked.

"There are no openings for the next three months. Based on what we read on the listing description, it appears they've been taking care of the rental themselves, meaning they don't go through an agency."

"If that's the case, either Eddy or Rosalyn paused the listing. And since Eddy's dead, my money's on Rosalyn. I stopped by her house earlier today. She wasn't home, and my mother said she hadn't seen any sign of her."

"If she had something to do with Eddy's death, I'll bet she's on the run. Seemed like such a sweet lady when I talked to her.

Shame. First Cordelia, then her husband ... would have never pegged her as a murderer."

"I wonder why Eddy's body was left in the garage."

"I'll tell you. During the power outage, we believe a refrigerator they kept in the garage short-circuited. When the electricity came back on, the refrigerator did not. As it thawed out, the door popped open. It's an old fridge. When we inspected the seal, we noticed it was worn."

"Have you determined Eddy's cause of death?" I asked.

"Not yet. As of now, there's nothing to explain what happened to him. There were no visible wounds of any kind and no signs of a struggle, nothing to explain how he ended up in that refrigerator."

"I'm guessing you don't know how long Eddy's been dead yet."

"We aren't sure, but Silas is working on it."

"It makes a lot more sense to me now. I talked to Eddy's boss today. He left a Rolex watch behind in his locker. Even if he quit his job, he would have come back for a watch like that. Now we know why he didn't."

"Seems so, and now to the bigger question. Where's Rosalyn? And what's her involvement in Eddy's and Cordelia's murders?"

When I woke the next morning, my thoughts were on Eddy, how he died, why he died, and whether it was at the hands of Rosalyn. Was she responsible for the two murders, and if so, was she on the run? I believed she was, and given Foley had put out an APB the night before, I hoped it wouldn't be long before they found her.

I stepped out of the shower, toweled off, grabbed my cell phone, and texted Simone and Hunter, asking them to meet me at the office in an hour. As I set the phone back down on the nightstand, my focus shifted to the book I'd taken from Cordelia's house. The Agatha Christie novel, *The Pale Horse*, which held Cordelia's snooping notes, was one I'd read decades earlier, but I'd forgotten a large portion of the plot.

Staring down at it now, a thought occurred to me. Was it possible Cordelia chose the book for a reason? Did it hold significance? Could it be tied to her murder somehow?

I altered my plans, canceling the meeting with Simone and Hunter, and letting them know I'd reschedule with them later in the day. I slipped into a pair of comfy pajamas and returned to bed, spending the next several hours poring over the classic novel.

In *The Pale Horse*, several residents in a quaint village in London were found dead. The deaths seemed to be of natural causes at first, but many of the deceased had one thing in common. Prior to their death, their hair had started falling out. In the end, as it was with many of Agatha's murder mysteries, the reader learns the victims had been poisoned.

Thallium, which had no taste, no color, and was water-soluble, was almost impossible to detect. A poison so toxic, it had been banned in the United States since 1965 for household use and since 1975 for commercial use.

Given it was difficult to get one's hands on the poison nowadays, it would be a stretch to think anyone had murdered a person in such a way. But it hadn't *always* been illegal—in fact, it had one been the main ingredient in rat poison.

My mind was racing, connecting several dots at once:

The book.

The notes contained within it.

The fact there were no signs of a struggle when Eddy was found.

The fact it wasn't clear how he died.

The shelf in Eddy and Rosalyn's shed with a distinct square impression, leading me to believe something on it had been removed not too long ago.

Thallium may have been banned since the mid-'60s, but Rosalyn's house was built much earlier. It was possible the people who owned the home prior to Rosalyn and Eddy had kept thallium-based rat poison in the shed and had never disposed of it before selling their house.

To test my theory, I needed some advice. I messaged Silas, asking if he could meet me at Rosalyn's house. He was hard at work on Eddy's autopsy but agreed to break away in a couple of hours. We set a time, and I made a new plan. I called Hunter, asking her to find out who owned the house prior to Rosalyn and Eddy. She got back to me in minutes with an answer— Lorena and Alexander Potts.

Since selling their home, Lorena and Alexander had moved to a retirement community, which wasn't far from my house. I made the drive over, and when I reached the door, it was opened by a short, curly, gray-haired woman, wearing a brown apron with wine bottles all over it. She had a sweet smile and an inquisitive look on her face.

"Hello," she said.

"Hello, my name is Georgiana Germaine. Are you Lorena Potts?"

"I sure am."

"I understand you sold your house to Rosalyn and Eddy Westwood."

"We did sell the house to them, yes. Nice couple ... well, Rosalyn was an absolute charmer. The husband, not so much. Had a bit of a foul mouth on him. Why do you ask?"

"I am a private investigator working on Cordelia Bennett's case, your former neighbor."

Lorena frowned. "Yes, I read all about it in the paper. What a horrible thing to happen to such a nice woman. What can I do for you?"

"I was hoping I could ask you and your husband a few questions."

"I'm happy to speak with you, but I'm afraid my husband won't be joining us. He died last year, you see."

"I'm sorry. I didn't know."

"Oh, it's all right, honey. He gave me the best sixty years of my life. I know I'll see him again, and when I do, we have all eternity to be together. Would you like to come inside?"

"I would."

"Wonderful. It just so happens I baked a tray of blueberry muffins not fifteen minutes ago. I like to take treats to some of my neighbors when I can. Most are not as agile as me in their old age. I'd like to think a sweet treat makes their day."

She'd said it with a wink, full of pride, as she should have been.

I'd never been a fan of muffins of any kind. When I did have one, I sliced it in half, eating the muffin top and discarding the rest, which was wasteful and why I didn't eat them often. But since I'd been offered a muffin by such a kind woman, saying no was out of the question.

Lorena plated a muffin for each of us, and we walked to her sitting room. A beautiful, pink-floral teapot rested on a table with four teacups next to it.

"I've just brewed a pot of Lady Grey," she said. "I'll pour us both some, and you can tell me more about why you're here."

She poured the tea and sat it on a side table next to me.

"The reason I wanted to speak to you is because I was in your old shed yesterday," I said. "On one of the shelves, it looked like something had been removed not too long ago. Did you leave anything behind when you moved out?"

"If we did, I wouldn't know. The shed was my husband's domain. I never much cared to go in there."

"Do you know whether your husband kept anything containing thallium in the shed at one time?"

"I'm not even sure what thallium is, if I'm being honest."

"It's a poison, and it was banned in the 60s. Before then, it was one of the ingredients in rat poison."

Lorena crossed one leg over the other, sipped a bit of tea, and said, "Rat poison, you say? Well then, yes, it's possible. If I remember right, we did have a big rat problem one year. My husband went to the store and brought back a large tin of Reeds Rat Killer. I remember it well because the label on the front was a cartoonish rat in a coffin. I have no idea if it contained thallium, but it may have. All I can tell you is it worked. We were free of rats after that."

I sent Hunter a text, giving her the name of the rat poison, and I asked her to see what she could find out about it. Then I returned my attention to Lorena. We chatted for a while longer while I finished my tea and muffin. Then I thanked her for her time. As I was heading out, she stopped me, saying, "Might I ask why you were inquiring about the rat poison?"

I considered what response I wanted to give and landed on one of honesty. "I'm sorry to say that Eddy Westwood was found dead last night. Since his death is being investigated, I can't go into all the details, but it's possible he was poisoned."

"I would hate to think something we bought contributed to another's death, but I thank you for telling me."

"One last question before I go," I said. "Were you friends with Cordelia?"

"Good friends, yes."

"Do you know if she was ever in your shed while you lived there?"

Lorena considered the question. "She was, yes. Marlon and Cordelia would come over from time to time, asking to borrow some of my husband's tools."

"You've been a great help to me, Lorena," I said.

She opened the front door, and as she wished me a good day, she said, "Are you getting close to finding Cordelia's killer?"

I looked at her, smiling as I said, "Yes, I believe I am."

I was with Silas, in Eddy and Rosalyn's backyard.

"A dead body can last three to four weeks in a refrigerator," Silas said.

"And then?" I asked.

"Refrigeration slows down the decomposition process, but it doesn't stop it. Eddy had a lot of bloating, and he'd gone red, which tells me he'd been in there for a couple of weeks, at minimum. If he was in there longer, his teeth and nails would have started fallin' out, and he'd start to liquefy."

"Gross," I said.

"Yeah, I know, sorry."

Today Silas was wearing a button-up, rayon shirt with surfboards all over it. The first four buttons were undone. He'd paired the shirt with black board shorts and flip flops.

"Where are you in your autopsy?" I asked.

"I've just started. What did you want to talk to me about?"

"This is going to sound a little far-fetched at first but stick with me. I believe I'm on the right track. And while I still don't know how Eddy's murder is connected to Cordelia's, I hope knowing how he died will provide me with answers."

"First, I don't believe anything you've ever said to me has sounded farfetched. It's much the opposite. No matter how unique your theories are, they're almost always correct."

"And second?"

"If you believe you know how Eddy died, it will be my personal mission to help you prove it."

I threw my arms around him. "And this is why we're such good friends."

"Not good friends ... *great* friends."

We made our way to Rosalyn and Eddy's shed and stepped inside. I walked over to the shelf, turned on my phone's flashlight, and pointed at the shelf, saying, "I was in here yesterday, and I noticed the entire shed is full of dust except for this square shape right here."

"Whatcha thinking?"

"I'm thinking there was something on this shelf, and it was removed in recent weeks. The questions running through my mind are: what was here, and why was something removed and not put back?"

"Have you come up with any answers?"

I raised a finger. "Why yes, I believe I have. It's my opinion that rat poison was on this shelf. I spoke with the previous owner of the house, and she confirmed they had a rat problem at one time, and her husband had bought a tin of Reeds Rat Killer. I asked Hunter to look it up, and she confirmed thallium was the main ingredient in the rat poison."

"This is all exciting news, but I have to ask, what makes you think Eddy was poisoned?"

"I have an interesting story to tell you."

"As always. But can you tell it outside of here? I'm not a fan of dark, dirty spaces."

I wasn't either.

We headed outside, and as we walked toward my car, I filled

him in. I told him about the notes I'd found, the Christie novel, the relevance of it, and how I believed it was connected to Eddy's murder.

When I finished, he said, "Fascinating, just one question."

"Shoot."

"Even if Cordelia knew about the rat poison in the shed, we don't know whether Rosalyn knew it was there or how it could be used to kill someone."

"Right, I think one of two things happened here. Cordelia poisoned Eddy, and maybe Rosalyn found out what she'd done and killed her."

"Or?"

"Rosalyn killed Eddy. It makes more sense, given he was found in their investment rental, a home I doubt Cordelia would have been able to access. In her notes, Cordelia said something about helping the person she was spying on. I'm thinking she told Rosalyn about the rat poison. It's possible she even explained how to use it."

"I'll get back to the lab and run a blood test on Eddy, see what I can find out."

I nodded, and as we said our goodbyes, my phone rang.

I answered with, "Hey, Whitlock, what's up?"

"Foley would like you to come to the police department. You available?"

"I sure am. What's going on?"

"We found Rosalyn Westwood, and she's refusing to talk to anyone but you."

Given Rosalyn and I hadn't hit it off during our previous conversations, I was unsure why she wanted to speak to me and only me.

When I arrived at the police department, I learned Rosalyn hadn't gotten far before she was found at a dive hotel about forty miles away. Whitlock said when they arrested her, she acted relieved, like she'd been sitting at the hotel, waiting for it to happen. He'd done his best to get her to talk on the drive to the station, but she'd said nothing. She'd sat in the back seat, clutching her dog, sobbing the whole way.

After she was brought in, Foley took a turn at getting her to open up. She still said nothing, so he decided to take the dog out of the room, promising the dog would be in good hands while she was questioned. It wasn't the nicest thing to do, but he seemed to believe it had led to her asking for me.

When I entered the interrogation room, the first thing I noticed was the pile of crumpled tissues on the table. Rosalyn's face was stained with tears, and she looked like she hadn't slept since the last time we talked.

The first thing she said to me was, "Have you seen Boomer? Is he all right?"

"I saw him when I came in, and he's just fine. The receptionist is keeping an eye on him, and he's snuggled up in her lap."

"What a relief. Can I get him back?"

"It's not up to me, but I will see if there's anything I can do."

She sniffled a soft, "Thank you."

I took a seat across from her. "I heard you wanted to talk to me."

"I just ... I didn't want to talk to *them*. I wanted to talk to a woman, someone who understands. The only one I could think of was you."

"I'm glad you asked for me. You can tell me anything. I'm here to listen."

"I guess you know about Eddy."

"I do. His body was found in your rental home last night."

"They think I killed him."

"*Did you* kill him?"

She leaned forward, burying her face in her hands. "It's all so complicated. Everything isn't always black or white."

In this instance, it was, though.

Either she murdered him, or she didn't.

"Do you want to tell me what happened?" I asked.

She went silent for a time. "Eddy wasn't always the man he was at the end."

"And what kind of man would that be?"

"Cold. Jealous. Aggressive. Demanding. When we first got together, I thought he was the funniest, kindest man I'd ever met. It didn't last long, not once we were married."

"What changed?"

"I couldn't tell you because I don't know. It was like a switch.

One day he was the person I'd married, and the next he was someone else, someone I didn't know anymore."

"Are you ready to be honest with me about the bruises I pointed out the other day? How long had he been abusing you?"

She paused a moment. "Too long ... far too long."

"Did you ever try to get away from him?"

"You read Cordelia's notes. You know I did, and you know what he did to me when he caught me."

"Did you ever tell anyone what he was doing to you?"

"I thought about telling my parents."

"Why didn't you?" I asked.

"My parents stopped talking to me after we got married. They were angry with me because I didn't listen to their warnings about him. They couldn't stand him. The thought of calling them up and telling them they were right ... it was just too hard. I was embarrassed to admit they'd been right all along.."

"Did Cordelia tell you she'd seen some of the interactions between you and Eddy?" I asked.

Rosalyn crossed her arms, shaking her head shaking as she said, "This is ... it's too much. I can't ... I don't want to talk about it anymore."

I felt certain I'd been close to a confession, but now she was stalling.

I pushed the chair back and stood. "Hey, I don't know about you, but I could go for a cold drink. Is there anything I can get you?"

"Can I have a glass of water?"

"You bet. I'll be right back."

I stepped out of the room, meeting Foley and Whitlock in the hall.

"Well," Foley said, "what are your initial thoughts?"

"I think I was close to a confession. I need the dog."

"The dog is a distraction," he said.

"The dog is all she cares about," I said. "She threw him a birthday party the other day. Trust me, the dog will bring her the comfort she needs right now."

"I'm with Georgiana on this," Whitlock said.

"Sure, sure," Foley said. "Gang up on me, why don't ya? Fine, get the dang dog and then get the conversation back on track."

I got us each a cup of water, took them back to the room, and then told her I needed to step out again for a minute. She shrugged, and I walked out, went to the receptionist's desk, and scooped Boomer into my arms.

Rosalyn's eyes lit up when I returned.

"Someone was missing his mom," I said.

She threw her arms up, and I handed Boomer off to her.

"I can't thank you enough," she said.

I could think of one way she could.

I sat back down, gave her a moment with Boomer, and then said, "If I leave here and we haven't finished our conversation, I'm not sure they'll let me talk to you again."

It was a half-truth.

I never knew when it came to Foley, but I had a good track record of being persuasive.

She cleared her throat once, then twice. "Guess I should start by saying, the day your sister saw me talking to Cordelia, it wasn't about the cat. I mean, I had issues with her cat, but it wasn't what we were talking about that day."

"Just so we're clear, I never believed your story."

A quick nod. "Okay, so Cordelia saw me outside, and she came over. She said she'd been trying to get me alone for days. It was then I learned she'd been watching us for some time. She'd seen the physical abuse, and she said she wanted to help me get away from Eddy."

"What did you say?"

"I refused her help, and she doubled down, telling me she'd

come up with a plan, a plan where I didn't have to live in fear because I'd never have to see him again."

"I believe I know the plan."

"How could you?"

"Can I suggest something to you, and you can tell me if I'm right?"

She shrugged. "I guess."

I opened my handbag, pulled out *The Pale Horse*, and slid it over to her.

"Why are you giving me a book?"

I tapped my finger on the book's cover. "This book is the one Cordelia kept the notes she'd taken about you and Eddy in. I didn't think much about it at first. This morning, I decided to read it, and I discovered something interesting. I now believe Cordelia chose this book for a specific reason."

"What reason?"

"Cordelia knew about the rat poison in your shed, the poison the previous owners left behind after they sold the house to you."

She blinked at me but said nothing.

"Rat poison used to contain thallium, a fact I believed Cordelia knew well. I had no doubt she'd read the Christie novel. And Lorena, the previous owner, admitted Cordelia been in their shed. I'm betting she saw the poison, knew how it worked, and that it was hard to trace. I think she saw it as a way for you to escape. When she came to you with an idea, I believe she suggested you poison him, and she told you how to do it. How am I doing so far?"

Her eyes flooded with tears.

I grabbed some tissues and handed them to her.

"Take all the time you need," I said. "I'm sure this is hard, and I'll bet you're scared. Trust me when I say it's better to be honest and come clean than it is to keep a difficult secret or live a life on the run."

"I never planned on things going this way, not until the power went out at the rental house. And then I panicked. I went over there the day after, and I saw that the refrigerator door was open. I couldn't get it to close again no matter what I did. At first I thought about wrapping a bungee strap around it, but the more I thought about it, the more paranoid I became. I was scared, and so I did the first thing that came to mind."

"You ran."

"I ... I did. My original plan was to move Eddy after a few days to somewhere he would never be found. Every time I went to do it, I lost my nerve. And as the days passed, I worried he was starting to decompose, and I didn't know what I'd see when I opened that door again."

"Did you think killing him was your only way out?" I asked.

"If you knew him, you'd understand. He wouldn't have ever let me go. Even if I managed to get away, he'd find me. I didn't want to believe Cordelia's idea was the right one at first. In the end, it came down to one thing—I either ended him, or I ended myself. I did what I had to do to save myself."

I took a sip of water and thought about what to say next. "Going back to the beginning, I just want to make sure I have it right. Did you poison him?"

"I ... yes."

"Tell me about it."

"Cordelia suggested I give Eddy a little bit of poison, not too much, just a little, each day. Every morning for six days, I put it in his coffee. Several days passed and nothing happened, and I didn't think it would work. I thought the poison was too old, or his body handled it a lot better than I thought it would, or that I hadn't given him enough of it. On the seventh day, I woke up, and he didn't."

"Was it always your plan to keep him in the refrigerator at your rental house?"

She shook her head. "Cordelia gave me the idea. On the day he died, I waited until nightfall, and then I pulled my car into the garage. I put Eddy in the trunk, and I drove to the rental. My plan was to leave him there for no more than a few days. Cordelia was going to help me figure out what to do next."

"And then she was murdered."

She nodded. "And I lost it."

"Did you have anything to do with Cordelia's death?"

"No."

"Do you have any idea who killed her or why?"

"If I did, I would tell you."

Rosalyn had lied to me before.

What was stopping her from lying to me again?

She gave her dog a squeeze and said, "What's going to happen to me?"

"Foley and Whitlock will come in and take your confession. You need to hire a lawyer, a good one. Do you have someone?"

"N-no."

I grabbed my wallet out of my handbag, fishing out a business card. I stood and handed it to her. "Tiffany Wheeler is a friend of mine. We went to school together. She's good. You can trust her."

Rosalyn thanked me, adding, "You know the saddest thing of all? A life in prison is refreshing after all I've been through. It'll be far less of a hell than the life I would have spent living with him. Because he would never have let me go."

35

When I entered Foley's office after my interview with Rosalyn, he was standing next to Whitlock, talking about her confession. They looked over at me, smiled, and Whitlock let out a long whistle.

"Way to go in there," Foley said. "You sure there's no way I can talk you into coming back and working for me?"

"I'm sure but thank you."

"We have one confession. Now we just need to get the other one out of her. Any ideas?"

I moved a hand to my hip. "You don't think she committed both murders do you?"

"I sure do. Don't you?"

"No, I don't."

"Why not? Given she had a relationship with both victims, it seems obvious."

"The murders were nothing alike. And then there's the note Whitlock found in the library, which suggests someone was hired to kill Cordelia."

"We've never been able to confirm the note has anything to do with the case."

We hadn't disproved it either.

"Then you have Eddy, who was poisoned over the course of a week and then stuck in a refrigerator," I said. "Their deaths seem too different to be connected."

"The connection is Rosalyn. The way I see it, the woman killed her husband, and then she either hired someone to murder her neighbor, or she took care of it herself."

"Why would she kill Cordelia, the one person who was trying to give her a way out, a new life, without Eddy in it?"

Foley shook his head. "Was it a way out? What if, after Rosalyn murdered her husband, she worried Cordelia might let it slip, tell someone what she'd done? Rosalyn could have wanted to tie up loose ends."

"As a murderer, she's awful at it," I said. "Think about it, Foley. If she was going to hire someone to kill Cordelia, why wouldn't she hire someone to kill her husband as well, instead of killing him herself?"

Foley turned to Whitlock. "You're being quiet for a change. Care to chime in?"

Whitlock raised a brow. "Rosalyn hasn't confessed to Cordelia's murder. It seems there may be a few more rocks that need to be turned over before we know what happened for certain."

"I spoke to Samantha yesterday, the woman who runs the library," I said. "She told me on the day Cordelia was murdered, a strange man came in."

"Well, this is news to me," Foley said. "When were you going to tell us?"

"Last night," I said. "And then you dropped the Eddy bombshell, and I decided it could wait."

"Hang on a minute. Start from the beginning. What did Samantha say?"

"On the afternoon of Cordelia's death, a man came into the library who Samantha found suspicious."

"Suspicious in what way?"

"He sat in the corner, pretending to read a book while looking around, watching who was coming and going. She tried to start a conversation with the man, and he wasn't interested. Afterward, she walked away. When she went back to check on him later, he was gone. No one saw him after that."

"What do you know about this man?"

"Samantha gave me a description, and that's all I have to go on right now. And there's one other thing. At the time the man was in the library, Cordelia was talking to Johnny, the other employee. I learned this information from Samantha. I talked to Johnny about their conversation, and he let it slip that it was more of an argument. I found it interesting because Samantha didn't describe their interaction as an argument at all."

"Do you know what the argument was about?"

"According to Johnny, Cordelia wanted to change the way they did things at the library. He wanted things to stay as they were. He didn't go into specifics, just something about getting the community more involved, and he didn't think they had a large enough community to justify the funding."

"See, it's just as I suggested," Whitlock said. "We're not done investigating. Let's kick a few more stones. We're close to solving the case. I can feel it."

36

I was sitting in my mother's living room, talking to her and Harvey about the investigation.

"Well, I'll be," my mother said. "You think you know a person, and to think it all happened on our quiet little street."

"Hard for me not to feel sorry for Rosalyn," Harvey said. "If she was being abused by her husband, and she felt she couldn't get out of the situation, she did what any animal does when it's caught in a trap."

"I feel the same way about the situation," I said. "There are those who wouldn't have sympathy for what she did, but none of us know the hell she went through with him."

"What about Cordelia?" my mother asked. "You don't think Rosalyn had anything to do with her death, do you?"

"I don't, and it's where Foley and I differ. He believes she's responsible for both murders. I don't see a strong enough connection."

"Well then," my mother said patting me on the knee, "I guess your job isn't done yet, is it?"

"It's not, and I'm not sure where to go from here."

"You'll figure it out, dear. You always do. Care to stay for dinner?"

"Sure, I'm on my own tonight."

"Where's that strapping young man of yours?"

"Giovanni is out of town, meeting with his cousin to talk about a new business venture. He'll be back in the morning."

"Wonderful. I made some lasagna last night. I have plenty left over for the three of us. I'll whip up a quick salad, and we'll be all set. Come, help me set the table."

I followed her to the kitchen, where I noticed the entire countertop was covered in photos.

"What are these?" I asked.

"It's my fun pet project. While helping Octavia, I've been taking photos here and there when I can, trying to preserve campaign memories for her. Once she gets voted into office again, I'll put together a little scrapbook, give it to her as a gift."

"I'm sure she will appreciate it."

My mother handed off some plates, silverware, and napkins, and I set the table.

While she made the salad, I returned to the counter, browsing through the photos. As I glanced at the first few rows, something caught my eye—or rather, someone.

I picked up one of the photos and turned it toward my mother, pointing at it. "Have you ever seen this man before?"

"Oh, yes. Let me think. Dustin something. Clement or Clemus ... Wait, no. It's Clemens. Dustin Clemens. Nice fellow."

"When and where was this photo taken?"

She gave the question some thought. "I'm not sure. Would have been in the last month. I believe Octavia was speaking in Magnolia Park that day. Have you been there since they made all the wonderful improvements? The bathrooms are gorgeous, nicer than mine. Why do you ask?"

"How do you know Dustin? And how does he relate to the events you've been attending?"

My mother tapped a finger to her cheek, thinking. "Come to think of it, I'm not sure. We never got that far in our conversation. It was a combined event."

"What do you mean?"

"Both candidates were speaking."

"Benjamin was there?"

"If it's the one I'm thinking of, yes. I've been to so many functions over the last month, they're all blending together."

"Have you ever taken Cordelia to an event?"

My mother tipped her head to the side and said, "Yes, I took her to a few. I was trying to get her out of the house."

My heart was racing, thoughts running in and out, puzzle pieces connecting at long last.

"Listen, Mom, I know I said I would stay for dinner, but I just remembered that there's an errand I forgot to run. Is it okay if I step out for a bit? Save me a plate, and I'll be back."

"Sure, I can, but dinner's almost ready. Why don't you have a seat, and you can run your errand after?"

I grabbed my handbag off the counter, slipped the photo of Dustin inside, and sprinted toward the door. "I would if I could, but this errand is one that cannot wait."

I drove to Samantha's house and showed her the photo. She was almost certain the man in it was the same person she'd seen at the library the day Cordelia died. We discussed Johnny and why she hadn't told me about his argument with Cordelia. She said she found it irrelevant—Johnny had nothing to do with the murder, in her mind, so she saw no reason to mention it.

My next stop was my office, and I was happy to find Hunter at her desk. I sat beside her, and we did a search on Dustin Clemens. What I learned shocked me.

I left the office and called Whitlock, telling him about the photo and how I believed Dustin was the man who'd murdered Cordelia. Whitlock said he'd bring him in for questioning, but before we ended the call, I asked him for a favor, telling him I'd explain why later. I had one last stop to make, and I wasn't looking forward to it.

I parked in front of a stylish, modern-style house. When I knocked on the door, a voice inside said, "Come on in. It's open."

I slid my hand inside my bag, palming my gun, thinking it was a good idea. I was protecting myself. Turned out, it was a mistake. A big mistake. As I walked through the front door, I realized I wasn't the only one with a gun, and the other gun was pointed right at me.

"I hoped it wouldn't come to this, Georgiana," Octavia said. "Although I think I always knew it would, ever since you were hired to investigate Cordelia's murder. You've always been too smart for your own good. Take a seat."

I did as she requested, and I considered my next move.

"What's your plan?" I asked. "Are you going to kill me, your good friend's daughter? Do you think you'd get away with it if you did? You wouldn't. My mother would live and breathe to catch my killer, and you know it."

She let out a long sigh. "This isn't what I wanted, any of it. I wish I could go back, but it's too late for all that now."

Octavia took a seat across from me, the gun still aimed at my chest. "I'm guessing you have a lot of questions for me."

"If I ask them, are they going to be answered?"

"Perhaps."

"You were waiting for me. How did you know I was coming?"

"Your mother called right after you left. We got to chatting, and she told me you'd been looking at the photos she'd taken. You made an excuse about having an errand to run. She didn't believe it was just an errand, but she didn't put it together. And why would she? She has no idea about my involvement."

"My mother has looked up to you for years," I said. "When she finds out what you did, she'll be devastated."

"Not when she finds out ... *if* she finds out, and she won't. As you were leaving her house, she saw you slip the photo of Dustin into your bag. She said you had a look on your face, the same look you get when you're about to solve a murder. I assumed you'd put enough together to come for me, and I was right. I also know what you're like, and I knew I'd have a little time to figure things out before you turn me in."

"And what am I like?"

Octavia crossed one leg over the other. "You prefer to solve a murder before you bring the police into it. You like to be sure. You pride yourself on it. I doubt they know you suspect me, not yet."

She'd pegged me well, but she hadn't gotten it *all* correct, a fact I decided to keep to myself until the time was right.

"What I still don't understand is why you had Cordelia killed in the first place," I said.

"What makes you think *I* had her killed?"

"After Cordelia was murdered, a piece of paper was found in the library with a description of a woman. It was a perfect match to Cordelia. That same day, the library manager saw a strange man lurking around. The man was your buddy—

Dustin."

She furrowed her brow, looking irritated. "Oh, for heaven's sake. How could he be so sloppy? If you want something done right, you have to do it yourself. No matter. In terms of evidence, I'm afraid you're falling a bit flat."

"I'm not done yet. Once I confirmed Dustin was in the library the day Cordelia died, I went to the office. I did some digging on him, and I'm sure you can imagine what I found out. Seems he's been putting out fires for you for a long time, which isn't a surprise since he works for you."

She rolled her eyes, grunting, "I should have never asked him for help."

"You still haven't told me why you had Cordelia killed, but I'd like to venture a guess. Cordelia saw something she shouldn't have, and she was murdered because of it."

"She's a nosey little thing—well, she *was* a nosey little thing."

"What happened at the park?"

"The gathering went as planned, and afterward, everyone left. I stayed behind for a while. I thought everyone had gone, but later I learned Cordelia, who'd come with your mother, had also stayed behind to go for a walk."

"That still doesn't explain why she's dead."

"I made a mistake, a foolish one, and Cordelia happened to be in the wrong place at the wrong time when I made it."

We stared at each other for a time. Though she was the one with the gun in her hand, the perspiration gathering around her forehead suggested she wasn't as confident as she wanted me to believe.

"What was the mistake?" I asked.

"I fooled around with a man, and I got caught in the middle of it."

"Fooled around with a man who wasn't your husband, you mean."

She nodded. "It wasn't my finest moment, and I figured it wasn't a big deal. It was a one-time thing. I'd decided it wouldn't happen again."

"When I was at my mother's house earlier, she was raving about the renovations in the park. In particular, the bathrooms. If I had to guess, I'd say your rendezvous happened there, and Cordelia caught you in the act."

"It's all *his* fault. He said he'd locked the door, and maybe he thought he had. In any case, she walked in, saw me with my dress hiked up, him with his pants down, going at it."

"And because of what she saw, you thought it warranted murdering her?"

"I didn't give it much thought, at first. I figured, she was a little old woman. I'd speak to her about it, and everything would be fine. It wasn't until she threatened me that I knew talking with her wouldn't work."

"She threatened you how?"

"You'd think the woman caught me murdering someone. She lectured me about how wrong it was to cheat on my husband, and when I laughed it off, her anger escalated. She decided I needed to make a public statement about it, admitting what I did. If I refused, she would make one herself. She said she'd seen a lot in her life, and she was tired of people not paying for their sins."

"What did you tell her?" I asked.

"I told her she could say whatever she liked, and no one would believe her."

"You didn't believe it, though."

"I believed it when I said it. Later, when I met up with Dustin, he saw how shaken up I was, and he asked me what was wrong."

"Did you tell him?"

"Not at first, but I've never been able to hide things from him. He knows me too well. There's nothing he wouldn't do for me. So, yes, I confided in him. When he had the full story, he said to leave it to him. He promised to be discreet, and he said he'd make it all go away."

"Did you even ask what he meant by that?"

She shook her head. "If you want the truth, I didn't want the details. I was better off not knowing."

"Not having the details still gets your hands dirty. You must have known what he was thinking about doing, and you didn't stop him from doing it."

"I knew. I just had no idea how indiscreet he was until now. What a fool ... what an absolute fool I've been."

"And the man you had sex with ... I don't need you to give me his name. I already know it—Benjamin Branson."

"Bravo."

"Before, when you said I prided myself on solving murders on my own, you're right. I do. This time, there's one exception." I held up my phone, turning it toward her. There, on the screen, was the photo I'd asked Whitlock to send. A photo of Dustin being questioned at the department by Foley. "They didn't know how you were involved. Now they do."

"Dustin will never turn on me."

"We'll see."

She scoffed, swished a hand through the air. "I already have a plan. I'll set up Benjamin to take the fall. It will be easy—too easy."

"You shouldn't be so confident."

"Enough talking. Stand up. We're going for a drive."

As I stood and readied myself to tackle her, Octavia's front door blew open, and my mother stormed in, gun in hand.

Eyes wild, she glared at Octavia, saying, "How dare you raise a gun to my daughter! Put it away this instant, Octavia, or I'll put a hole in your head."

38

I was sitting at my office desk, chatting with neighbor Kayla about the Cordelia Bennett murder investigation.

"How does it feel now that it's over?" she asked.

"Bittersweet," I said. "It was sad to learn the reason Cordelia was killed. I'm glad it's all over. Octavia and Dustin are behind bars where they belong."

"And your mother ... she saved the day, didn't she?"

I laughed. "She's still talking about it to anyone who will listen."

"She said she reached out to the two ladies you work with, after you left her house, and they knew you were going to talk to Octavia."

I nodded. "It was then she put it all together."

"I'm sure Cordelia's sister is relieved to know what happened."

"Claudette is an interesting woman. She went from refusing to make amends with her sister to deciding to move into Cordelia's house. She believes being there will make a difference somehow."

"I'm not sure I'm thrilled to have her as a neighbor, but time will tell."

"Tell me, how are things with you and Seth?"

She crossed her arms. "I don't know what you said to him, but ever since he talked to you that night he went to your house, he's been a different person. A kinder, happier person. He's even in therapy, which I never thought he would agree to do, and he's taking steps in the right direction. Baby steps, but steps all the same, to improve our marriage."

"I see you're wearing your wedding ring." She hadn't been when we first spoke all those weeks ago. "How are you feeling about it all? Is this what you want?"

"I thought I wanted out of the relationship, but I didn't. I was lying to myself. What I want is a version of him that's more supportive of me and what I need from a partner."

"Do you feel that you're getting that now?"

"In many ways, yes. I can tell it's a little hard on him. He's pushing himself out of his comfort zone for me. I'm learning to be patient and how to help and support him during this time of change."

I smiled. "I'm glad the two of you are getting things back on track."

"What about you? Your mom says you're planning a wedding? How exciting."

"Next year, in August. We've known each other for a long time, since college. It's taken a while to get us here, but I'm so glad we're in the right place at the right time now."

"I love a good love story." She stood, thanking me again for being the bridge back to her marriage, even though I didn't feel I'd done as much as she believed I had. We said our goodbyes, and she left the office. As soon as the door closed, it opened again. I looked up, assuming it was Giovanni, picking me up for our lunch date.

I was wrong.

"I've been meaning to stop by for weeks now," Benjamin said.

"Why?"

"I wanted to congratulate you on solving Cordelia's murder."

"If you and Octavia hadn't fooled around that day, Cordelia would still be alive. Perhaps you should wipe that smug smile off your face when you're talking to me about an innocent dead woman who was my mother's friend."

"I didn't mean to say it in a celebratory way. I'm sorry."

I'd grown tired of his apologies, and of him.

"You've said what you came to say," I said.

"Not all of it. I didn't know about Octavia's plan to have Cordelia murdered."

"I know. She said as much when she confessed."

"I guess what I want to say is, I know what I did was wrong. I justified it at the time because I'm not married."

"But you knew she was, and she was your opponent on top of it all."

"You're right. I ... I wasn't sure if you heard the news."

"I heard. Despite what happened, you'll still be mayor."

"Which brings me to the other reason I'm here. I'd like to be more involved in your investigations—in particular, homicides."

I tossed my head back, laughing. "No, thank you."

"Let me try again. What I mean to say is I'd like to help. I'm at your disposal. If there is ever anything you need, just ask."

I assumed his offer was made because of the guilt he felt.

I didn't need his help, and I never would.

"I'll keep it in mind," I said. "Is that all?"

"Almost. Is there a place in this world where the two of us could become friends?"

The man didn't know when to quit.

"I doubt it," I said.

"I would like to think we could find a way."

"I don't see how."

"I know I have a long way to go before I make things right with you. All I ask is for one more chance."

I crossed my arms, tapping a foot on the floor, thinking. Before I was able to respond, Giovanni walked in. He looked at Benjamin and then at me. "Are you ready?"

"I am. Benjamin was just leaving."

Benjamin walked toward Giovanni, extending his hand. "I'm Benjamin Branson. I don't believe we've met."

Giovanni shook hands with him. "No, we haven't."

Benjamin stood there, waiting for Giovanni to say something else. When he didn't, the silence became awkward, and then he did what I'd been longing for—he excused himself.

After he was gone, Giovanni turned to me. "What was that all about?"

"Nothing, really," I said. "Nothing but little empty promises."

THE END

Thank you for reading Little Empty Promises, book ten in the *USA Today* bestselling Georgiana Germaine mystery series.

I hope you enjoyed getting to know the characters in this story as much as I have enjoyed writing them for you. This is a continuing series with more books coming before and after the one you just read. You can find the series order (as of the date of this printing) in the "Books by Cheryl Bradshaw" section below.

. . .

In Little Hidden Fears, book 11 in the series:

Noelle Winters has just thrown the perfect engagement party ... or so she believes.

As the evening winds down and the toast is about the commence, the lights go out. And for someone, the night has just turned deadly.

What Readers are Saying about the Series:

*"Makes you **want to keep reading** the story into the night."*

*"A strong lead character and plenty of drama, it **keeps the reader engaged."***

*"Leaving you **wanting to read more."***

*"I **will definitely read more** from this author."*

*"Kept me on the **edge of my seat."***

. . .

———

Want a sneak peek? Here's an exclusive look at chapter one ...

LITTLE HIDDEN FEARS

LITTLE HIDDEN FEARS
CHAPTER 1

Noelle Winters slipped in between the guests, humming to herself as she scooped up a few empty plates off the table and walked to the kitchen. Handing them off to one of the staff members she'd hired for the evening, she moved a hand to her hip, reminiscing over the night's events.

The party was winding down now, a fact she was pleased about. Over the last hour, her feet had begun to hurt, making her wish she hadn't worn heels in the first place. She wanted nothing more than to kick them off and go barefoot for the remainder of the evening. And given most attendees were at least a few wines in, she doubted anyone would notice, or care, for that matter.

Six months of party planning had all come down to tonight, throwing the perfect engagement party for Zoe, her best friend since grade school. It was hard to believe a year ago Zoe was single and had announced she'd sworn off men for life. Noelle hadn't believed a word of it. And sure enough, Zoe retracted the statement the second she laid eyes on the debonair Lucas Bronson.

After a whirlwind, three-month romance, Lucas proposed,

and Zoe said yes. Over the next several months, they planned their wedding. In a few short weeks, they'd marry, move in together, and begin their new life in Cambria, California.

Thinking about it now, it was hard for Noelle to believe how much had changed in so little time.

But Zoe was happy, which was all Noelle had ever wanted.

A hand brushed across Noelle's arm, and she turned to see a beaming Zoe standing next to her in a satin, champagne-colored, split-thigh dress. She recalled the day they'd gone shopping for it. Zoe must have tried on at least fifty dresses that day. But when she stepped out of the dressing room in the one she wore now, they both knew their search had ended.

"I can't thank you enough for hosting my engagement party," Zoe said. "Every single moment tonight has been amazing."

Noelle smiled, saying, "If you're happy, I'm happy."

"I am. Hey, I haven't seen Lucas for a while. Have you?"

Noelle hadn't.

She'd been so focused on the party, there hadn't been much time to focus on anything else.

"Sorry, no. I've been preoccupied."

Zoe draped an arm around Noelle's neck. "I thought that's why you hired staff tonight, so you could relax and enjoy the party along with everyone else."

"I know, I know. I can't help it. I want everything to be perfect."

"It *is* perfect. Promise me you'll relax now."

"I promise I'll try."

"Where's Kiera? I haven't seen her much tonight either."

"Dominic took her up to bed about a half an hour ago. I bet he's still with her, helping her settle in for the night," Noelle said.

"Or hiding out somewhere upstairs. Your husband has never been comfortable in a room full of people."

Noelle shot Zoe a wink. "That's true, but when I suggested hosting the party here tonight, he was a good sport. I'm surprised he lasted as long as he did."

"I'm not. He'd do anything for you."

Almost anything.

"It's just about time for the toast," Noelle said. "And given the guests have gone through almost all of the champagne, I need to bring in some reinforcements."

"Should I send someone to get more bottles?"

"Not only do I have backups, I have backups for the backups."

They both laughed, and Noelle excused herself, heading upstairs to grab the additional bottles of champagne she'd stashed in her wine fridge upstairs. Along the way, she cracked open her daughter's door and peeked inside. Five-year-old Kiera was curled on her side, fast asleep, her favorite white teddy bear clutched in her arms. Dominic was nowhere in sight.

Noelle pulled the bedroom door closed and rounded the corner into the master bedroom. She made her way to the wine fridge and bent down. The moment she reached inside to grab the bottles, the lights went out, cloaking the room in darkness.

She heard gasps and cries of surprise from the guests downstairs as they bumped around, trying to find their way in the dark. Noelle thought she'd considered every possible scenario tonight but losing power had been the furthest thing from her mind.

Mind racing, she searched for a solution ... and then, clarity came. Each of the skinny, high-top tables she'd rented for the evening had been decorated with a candle in its center. All she needed was to grab the mini flashlight out of her desk drawer, locate the matches in the kitchen, and light the candles.

She stood and reached out, using her hands to feel her way along the wall toward her office. The moment she stepped inside, a strange sensation gripped her, like someone's hands around her neck. And then came the squeeze, a crushing pain unlike anything she'd ever felt before.

Noelle wrestled for breath, but breath didn't come, and as she struggled to maintain consciousness, every little hidden fear she'd ever had came collapsing down around her.

———

I hope you enjoyed the sneak peek!

Reserve your copy of Little Hidden Fears today at CherylBradshawStore.Com

ENJOY LITTLE EMPTY PROMISES?

You can show your appreciation by leaving a review on Amazon, Barnes & Noble, Apple Books, Google Play, Kobo, or Goodreads.

If you write a review, please be sure to email Cheryl (cheryl@authorcherylbradshaw.com) so she can express her gratitude. She does her best to reply to as many emails as she can, and she appreciates every piece of mail she receives.

About Cheryl Bradshaw

Cheryl Bradshaw is a New York Times and 11-time USA Today bestselling author writing in multiple genres, including mystery, thriller, romantic suspense, supernatural suspense, and poetry. She is a Shamus Award finalist for best private eye novel of the year, an eFestival of Words winner for best thriller, and has published over fifty books since 2011.

When she's not writing, Cheryl loves jet-setting to new countries, playing with her grandkids, high tea, and pursuing a wishful side career as a professional food tester of wine and cheese.

Never Miss One of Cheryl's Book's Again!

Sign up for Cheryl Bradshaw's "Killer Newsletter" today to be the first to know when a new book is released and to enter to win fun bookish swag. You'll also receive some fantastic book freebies just for joining!

Learn more by visiting CherylBradshawStore.Com

BOOKS BY CHERYL BRADSHAW

Sloane Monroe Series

Silent as the Grave (Prequel, Book 0)

When the body of Rebecca Barlow is found floating in the lake, private investigator Sloane Monroe takes on her very first homicide.

Black Diamond Death (Book 1)

Charlotte Halliwell has a secret. But before revealing it to her sister, she's found dead.

Murder in Mind (Book 2)

A woman is found murdered, the serial killer's trademark "S" carved into her wrist.

I Have a Secret (Book 3)

Doug Ward has been running from his past for twenty years. But after his fourth whisky of the night, he doesn't want to keep quiet, not anymore.

Stranger in Town (Book 4)

A frantic mother runs down the aisles, searching for her missing daughter. But little Olivia is already gone.

Bed of Bones (Book 5) (USA Today Bestselling Book)

Sometimes even the deepest, darkest secrets find their way to the surface.

Flirting with Danger (Book 5.5) A Sloane Monroe Short Story

A fancy hotel. A weekend getaway. For Sloane Monroe, rest has finally arrived, until the lights go out, a woman screams, and Sloane's nightmare begins.

Hush Now Baby (Book 6) (USA Today Bestselling Book)

Serena Westwood tiptoes to her baby's crib and looks inside, startled to find her newborn son is gone.

Dead of Night (Book 6.5) A Sloane Monroe Short Story

After her mother-in-law is fatally stabbed, Wren is seen fleeing with the bloody knife. Is Wren the killer, or is a dark, scandalous family secret to blame?

Gone Daddy Gone (Book 7) (USA Today Bestselling Book)

A man lurks behind Shelby in the park. Who is he? And why does he have a gun?

Smoke & Mirrors (Book 8) (USA Today Bestselling Book)

Grace Ashby wakes to the sound of a horrifying scream. She races down the hallway, finding her mother's lifeless body on the floor in a pool of blood. Her mother's boyfriend Hugh is hunched over her, but is Hugh really her mother's killer?

Sloane Monroe Stories: Deadly Sins

Deadly Sins: Sloth (Book 1)

Darryl has been shot, and a mysterious woman is sprawled out on the floor in his hallway. She's dead too. Who is she? And why have they both been murdered?

Deadly Sins: Wrath (Book 2)

Headlights flash through Maddie's car's back windshield, someone following close behind. When her car careens into a nearby tree, the chase comes to an end. But for Maddie, the end is just the beginning.

Deadly Sins: Lust (Book 3)

Marissa Calhoun sits alone on a beach-like swimming hole nestled on Australia's foreshore. Tonight, the lagoon is hers and hers alone. Or is it?

Deadly Sins: Greed (Book 4)

It was just another day for mob boss Giovanni Luciana until he took his car for a drive.

Deadly Sins: Envy (Book 5)

A cryptic message. A missing niece. And only twenty-four hours to pay.

Deadly Sins: Pride (Book 6)

A secret lies within the Kingston mansion's walls, a secret that's about to bring the past into the present.

Sloane & Maddie, Peril Awaits (Co-Authored with Janet Fix)

The Silent Boy (Book 1)

In the hallway of a local tavern, six-year-old Louie Alvarez waits for his mother to take him home. A scream rips through the air, followed by the sound of a gun being fired. Louie freezes, then turns, with a single thought on his mind: RUN.

The Shadow Children (Book 2)

Within the tunnels of the historic port city of Savannah, fourteen-year-old Andi Leland has her mind set on freedom—not just for herself but for all the other teens who have come before her.

The Broken Soul (Book 3)

When the party of a lifetime becomes a party to the death, the lines become blurred. Friends become enemies. Drugs become weapons. And that's just the beginning.

The Widow Maker (Book 4)

A friend murdered. A business in trouble. A marriage struggling to survive. And that's just the beginning.

Georgiana Germaine Series

Little Girl Lost (Book 1)

For the past two years, former detective Georgiana "Gigi" Germaine has been living off the grid, until today, when she hears some disturbing news that shakes her.

Little Lost Secrets (Book 2)

When bones are discovered inside the walls during a home renovation, Georgiana uncovers a secret that's linked to her father's untimely death thirty years earlier.

Little Broken Things (Book 3)

Twenty-year-old Olivia Spencer sits at her desk in her mother's bookshop, dreaming about her upcoming wedding. The store may be closed, but she's not alone, and her dream is about to become her worst nightmare.

Little White Lies (Book 4)

When a serial killer sweeps through the streets of Cambria, California, Georgiana Germaine gets swept up into a tangled web of deception and lies.

Little Tangled Webs (Book 5)

What if you knew the person you loved was murdered, but no one else believed you? Eighteen-year-old Harper Ellis knows she's right, and she's prepared to risk her life to prove it.

Little Shattered Dreams (Book 6)

At fifty-five, Quinn Abernathy has been through her fair share of experiences in life. And tonight, her past is coming back to haunt her.

Little Last Words (Book 7)

After living in a verbally abusive relationship for the past six years, twenty-seven-year-old Penelope Barlow has finally found the courage to leave. But can she escape ... with her life?

Little Buried Secrets (Book 8)

In a split-second, a car collides with Margot, and she finds herself hurdling through the air, her bike going one way as she goes the other. Her mind whirls in this moment, as she thinks about her life and just how much she doesn't want to die.

Little Stolen Memories (Book 9)

In a secluded cabin deep within the woods, an ominous stranger is about to change the lives of six unsuspecting teenagers forever.

Little Empty Promises (Book 10)

As librarian Cordelia Bennett prepares to lock up for the night, a mysterious sound startles her. She turns. The fading light reveals a chilling presence in the shadows, and Cordelia realizes she's not alone.

Little Hidden Fears (Book 11)

Noelle Winters has just thrown the perfect engagement party ... or so she believes. As the evening winds down and the toast is about the commence, the lights go out. And for someone, the night has just turned deadly.

Addison Lockhart Series

Grayson Manor Haunting (Book 1)

When Addison Lockhart inherits Grayson Manor after her mother's untimely death, she unlocks a secret that's been kept hidden for over fifty years.

Rosecliff Manor Haunting (Book 2)

Addison Lockhart jolts awake. The dream had seemed so real. Eleven-year-old twins Vivian and Grace were so full of life, but they couldn't be. They've been dead for over forty years.

Blackthorn Manor Haunting (Book 3)

Addison Lockhart leans over the manor's window, gasping when she feels a hand on her back. She grabs the windowsill to brace herself, but it's too late-- she's already falling.

Belle Manor Haunting (Book 4)

A vehicle barrels through the stop sign, slamming into the car Addison Lockhart is inside before fleeing the scene. Who is the driver of the other car? And what secrets within the walls of Belle Manor will provide the answer?

Crawley Manor Haunting (Book 5)

Something evil is coming. Something dark. Something seeking to destroy everything and everyone in its path. And Addison Lockhart is the only one who can stop it.

Till Death do us Part Novella Series

Whispers of Murder (Book 1)

It was Isabelle Donnelly's wedding day, a moment in time that should have been the happiest in her life...until it ended in murder.

Echoes of Murder (Book 2)

When two women are found dead at the same wedding, medical examiner Reagan Davenport will stop at nothing to discover the identity of the killer.

Stand-Alone Novels

Eye for Revenge (USA Today Bestselling Book)

Quinn Montgomery wakes to find herself in the hospital. Her childhood best friend Evie is dead, and Evie's four-year-old son witnessed it all. Traumatized over what he saw, he hasn't spoken.

The Perfect Lie

When true-crime writer Alexandria Weston is found murdered on the last stop of her book tour, fellow writer Joss Jax steps in to investigate.

Hickory Dickory Dead (USA Today Bestselling Book)

Maisie Fezziwig wakes to a harrowing scream outside. Curious, she walks outside to investigate, and Maisie stumbles on a grisly murder that will change her life forever.

Roadkill (USA Today Bestselling Book)

Suburban housewife Juliette Granger has been living a secret life ... a life that's about to turn deadly for everyone she loves.